The Devil Made Me

Cheryl Terra

Bang It Out Writing

Trigger + Content Warnings

This book explores heavier topics that some readers may wish to be aware of prior to reading. I have tried to address those topics here without spoiling the story, however if you have concerns about any of the items listed and wish to know more, please reach out to me via email at **info@cherylterra.com**.

The Devil Made Me is a M/M dramatic romance. It explores issues surrounding homophobia, religious trauma, homelessness, and toxic and abusive family situations including parental abandonment.

While mild, The Devil Made Me includes scenes with mild violence/fighting and homophobic language. It touches on aspects of depression and contains brief mentions of suicide.

One

I KNEW SOMETHING WAS off when Vincent greeted me like he *didn't* think I was the world's biggest asshole.

"Sean," he said, lengthening my name with a nauseatingly fake cheerfulness.

"Nope," I said, turning towards the coffee maker.

"Nope?" he repeated, chuckling. "Nope what?"

"Don't toy with me. What do you want?"

"Why do I have to want something? I can't just say hello to the latest rising star in the world of luxury architecture?"

"Ooh, rising star? You must really want something," I said. "So that's gonna be a hard nope, now."

"You don't even know what I'm asking for."

"And yet, I know you well enough to know that you're about to tell me about this client that my style would be absolutely *perfect* for, and isn't it so convenient that they're going to be coming in for a consult in, what, fifteen minutes?" I filled my mug and turned to him. "Little do I know this client is secretly a diva extraordinaire who may or may not be homophobic and is going to take one look at me, screech that they can't believe they've been stuck with some—oh, now, what was the phrasing..."

"Come on, Sean, it's—"

"... Oh, that's right! 'Underdeveloped curl-headed twink who won't be able to focus for ten seconds when my husband's in the room'—and demand that Leanne fire me for daring to wear a dress shirt that had buttons instead of cufflinks because 'what kind of cheap ass architecture firm am I paying for if your staff can't even bother to dress with some semblance of decency?'"

Silence hung awkwardly in the room.

"That was one time," Vincent finally said.

"Okay, what about the time with Max Belanger and you—"

"Technically, that was also just one time."

"Right, and the time you—"

"Look, we've both said some things and done some things in the past that maybe haven't worked out all that well," Vincent said hurriedly. "This time, I swear, Sean, the client's super easygoing. You won't even believe who it is. It might even get you to crack a smile, Mr. Grumpy Pants."

"You're not helping your case."

"Theo Barker."

I stared at him. "The singer?"

Vincent nodded, smiling like he was trying to sell water to a mermaid. "He's building a house with his wife or girlfriend or something. Really open to suggestions, lots of creative freedom, and a budget of 'does it look nice? Okay, do it.'"

"So what's the catch?"

"What?"

"Why are you trying to pawn him off on me?" I leaned against the break room counter. "Fool me once, shame on you. Fool me two... three... four times now? Come on, Vincent. What's the catch?"

He shook his head, raising his hands as if to show he had nothing to hide.

"No catch, man. I just don't have room on my plate for this and you know me, I'm a modern kinda guy. This Theo, he seems more like a..." He waved his hand in my general direction. "...you know. Your kinda style."

"Are you saying I'm not modern?"

He rolled his eyes. "You know what I mean. You're all about the rustic sort of feel. And classical looks. Real artsy stuff, you know? I'm all clean lines and gloss surfaces. This guy's a world-famous singer. He's gonna be all about the art, you know?"

I raised my eyebrows. "Have you ever *heard* a Theo Barker song?"

"'Course I have. He's popular."

"Good. You know his style as well as I do. Sounds like you've got it all figured out."

He almost growled in frustration. "Sean. Man. Look, I'm trying to be nice here."

"No you're not."

"I am." He held his arms out again. "I'm giving you the option to take this client off my plate. And this is a big client. This is the kind of stuff that gets your career *moving*, you know? And anyway, I'm allowed to assign you shit, so... you can either agree to take him on with all the accolades that come from being the project lead, or I can just say I need someone to take on the legwork while I take all the credit, you know?"

A spike of anger jolted through my chest, mostly because I knew he was right. I could feel heat rising up my neck and took a breath, trying to calm myself. "Fine."

"Fine?" Vincent repeated.

"I'll take your fucking client," I grumbled. "You're welcome."

He grinned, if it was possible to call the evil expression on his face a grin.

"C'mon, I'll bring you in and introduce you. He's waiting."

"Now?!"

I barely had time to grab my notebook and was frantically reading the chicken scratch Vincent had shoved into my hands as he led me down the hall. We got to the client meeting room, and before I could so much as ask him what "no beige or white but no colour" was supposed to mean, his hand was on the doorknob.

"Oh, by the way," he said.

"And here comes the catch," I muttered, still trying to take in the scribbled notes.

"The client is Theo Barker, but you'll be dealing with his personal assistant." He opened the door, his tone changing to the boisterous blast he used with clients. "Hey there! Sorry for the delay. There's been a change in who's going to lead your project."

I followed him into the room, only looking up when he finished speaking.

"Hi, I'm..."

I might have said my name. I might have also just trailed off. I knew my mouth was half-open as I looked at the man sitting at the table.

The most renowned sculptor in all of time and space couldn't have captured the chiselled lines of his face. It was almost unnatural how perfect his cheekbones were; the only reason I knew they were real was that there wasn't a surgeon alive who could've made them so symmetrical. A spattering of freckles dotted his cheeks and nose, only slightly darker than his skin tone, which was not as pale as one would expect for someone with hair like rust and copper and fire. It was styled neatly, brushed away from a strong forehead, and his eyes. They were the same shade of blue as the sky on a freezing winter day, the kind of day where the sun tricks you into thinking it's far warmer than it is, but the moment you step outside, you're frozen.

He was the most beautiful man I'd ever seen in my entire life, and he was looking straight at me.

Like something out of a dream, he unfolded his body from the chair he was sitting in, and I looked up, and up, and up at him. He was tall; six-four, maybe, at least six or seven inches taller than me, and dressed in jeans that made his legs look... well. I was definitely going to make a point of holding the door for him when we left the room.

"Sean?" he repeated.

Oh, good. I had said my name.

"Sean Lemieux," I repeated. "Nice to meet you, Mr., uh..." I glanced down at the papers in my hands. "... McDougall."

He smiled as he shook my hand and I almost lost it. "Just call me Rick."

I couldn't have stopped myself from grinning if I tried. "Sure thing, Rick."

Two

"HE'S A FUCKING NIGHTMARE," I said.

Mario fished the cherry out of his drink and popped it into his mouth. "I thought you said he was dreamy."

"He can be both." I rubbed my temple, where a muscle was twitching and throbbing. It wasn't painful so much as it was an annoyance, just like Rick fucking McDougall was.

"The pretty ones are always so much trouble," Breton said sympathetically, though his tone was about as genuine as the fillers in his lips.

"Like Sean would know."

Snickers circled the table as I glared at Pierre, whose pointed face was next to Armand's ear as though he'd muttered the words just for him. Armand was resting one muscled arm on the table, flexed in just such a way that the sleeve of his t-shirt was tight around his bicep. I imagined that was for the benefit of the "pretty ones" across the bar.

"Ha, ha," I said. "Like I haven't heard this from you a thousand times before."

"Well, I'm just saying." Pierre shrugged one shoulder gracefully. "You wouldn't be so cranky all the time if you'd just get laid once in a while."

"Aw, leave him alone," Armand said before I could give in to the temptation of anger. "Sean's a fine, upstanding young man who's just waiting for The One."

Unfortunately, that was just as annoying as what Pierre had said, and I glared at Armand.

"I'm not waiting for anything," I shot back. "I just don't need to hook up with random strangers to feel validated."

All of them hooted with laughter, even Armand, who apparently thought I was being playfully shady instead of honest.

"Mm, right." Pierre leaned forward and flicked the cross necklace I hadn't realized was peeking out from under my collar. "And you wear this because gold goes well with your skin tone or...?"

"Fuck off." I shoved his hand away and tucked the cross under my shirt, nearly shivering as the cool metal met scorching skin.

"I mean, it is a little weird," Breton said. "Like, do you go to church or...?"

"None of your business."

Pierre had an impishly intrigued look on his face.

"No, Seanie-bear, tell us." He leaned in again, folding his hands over each other on the table. "We've known you for, what, three years now? Time for you to open up."

"I'm good, thanks," I said uncomfortably.

"This is a safe space," he insisted. "Right, Armand?"

"Of course." Armand flexed and winked at me. "Anyone who says otherwise has to deal with me."

"Not what I meant, but that's the spirit!" Pierre wagged a finger at me. "Now, let us *finally* get to know you."

I stared at him for a moment. Everything about Pierre was thin; his features, his frame, and—as much as he tried to hide it—his hair. His slight stature was often buried beneath layers of trendy clothes and sparkling costume jewellery, and that night, he'd added a not-so-subtle touch of eyeliner to complete his "look," as he called it. He studied me with wide, insistent eyes and half a smirk playing on his lips.

From him I looked to Armand, the muscle head, who got most of his cardio by turning his many walks of shame into jogs of shame. His hair was cropped close to his head and he had huge brown eyes, and if it weren't for the fact that I knew he was a complete moron, I might have been attracted to him.

Then I glanced at Breton. He looked like he was trying to regain the appearance he had in his late twenties, which would have been fine, except he was in his early twenties. His expression was either curious or bored; given the amount of Botox in his forehead, I couldn't tell.

I didn't need to look at Mario to know what the expression on his round face looked like. He had tan skin and dressed impeccably well, but behind the sharpness of his collar and primness of his pressed shirts was one of the kindest people I'd ever met. I could feel his concern rolling off him, a protectiveness I knew meant he was trying to telepathically tell Pierre to back off.

At twenty-two, I was the youngest, though only a year younger than Breton. The four of them made up my friend group, and of them, I only actually liked Mario. The rest were more his friends than mine, but as I didn't have any friends, all of us put up with his insistence that I hang out with them. He seemed to think I needed a support circle, like I hadn't spent my whole life doing everything on my own, and since I owed everything to Mario, I obliged him when he said I needed to socialize with other people.

That didn't mean I was particularly good at it, though.

"I don't go to church anymore," I answered.

"But you, like, believe in God?" Breton asked.

"Sort of," I muttered.

Pierre pressed his lips together. "That's... interesting."

I looked at my glass of water, very aware of the four sets of eyes on me as a defensive sort of embarrassment curled in my chest.

"It's kind of personal," I said.

"So is that why you don't hook up with guys?" Armand asked.

"No," I said, glaring at him. "I told you, I just don't—"

"Yeah, yeah, we get it." Pierre waved a hand at me. "You're too good to whore around like the rest of us."

"I didn't say that." I could feel my pulse beating through my skin. "I just have other priorities."

"Of course," Breton said cheerfully. "We just want to make sure you're aware there's more to life than work and hockey and, uh, Jesus, apparently. But since you never *tell* us anything about you, how are we supposed to know?"

"Exactly," Pierre said. "Like, have you ever even had a boyfriend?"

"None of your business," I said before I could stop myself.

His thin eyebrows nearly touched his hairline. "Sean, for real? You've never had a boyfriend?"

"Oh my God," Armand said, looking at me with amazement. "Are you a *virgin*?"

"I am not," I said, my face turning red. "Just because I don't talk about—"

"You do, though," Pierre said. "You just told us about your dream-man-turned-nightmare."

My eyes darted from Armand to Pierre and back to the water glass just in front of me. "He was an annoying client who happened to be hot."

"Okay, then tell us," Pierre pressed. "How'd you lose your virginity?"

"I... it's not..." I stammered for a moment, hating how vulnerable I felt and how that vulnerability was just adding to the rage that was threatening to boil over.

Unfortunately, Breton took it to mean I was hiding something, and he slapped his hand on the table excitedly.

"Oh my *God*," he said, looking from me to Mario. "Did you two...?"

"No," Mario said patiently, though there was ice in his tone. "And seeing as it's pretty obvious that Sean doesn't want to talk about it—"

"Sounds like something someone who totally popped Sean's cherry would say," Pierre muttered to Armand.

A rushing sound filled my ears and I clenched a fist under the table, which didn't escape Mario's watchful gaze.

"Leave him alone," he snapped at the others.

"But it's just so fun to watch his face turn red," teased Armand.

"Oh, Sean knows we're just teasing." Pierre blinked at me innocently. "Right, Seanie-bear?"

Instead of doing what I wanted to do, which was push my chair away from the table and launch myself across it so I could feel Pierre's pointed nose crunch beneath my knuckles, I gritted my teeth and forced myself to reach for my glass of water. Beneath the table, Mario touched my knee, just subtle enough that the others wouldn't notice.

He knew just what I needed. There was nothing in his touch but concern. He hadn't been lying; we had only ever been friends, and we *definitely* hadn't... well, we hadn't had sex. In fairness, though, it had taken a drunken makeout session years earlier for us to realize there was nothing between us.

I loved him more than anyone else in the world. It just wasn't romantic love. I knew he felt the same way about me, mostly because we were in the middle of making out when he pulled back, looked at me, and said, "Sean, I love you, but this is fucking weird."

I burst out laughing and nodded. "Yeah, it's not... yeah."

He sighed dramatically and threw an arm around my shoulder, pulling me in so I could rest my head on him. "It's so unfair. You're gorgeous."

I smiled. "You are, too."

"Of course I am. We're both beautiful bottoms and that's why it can never work, my love."

He nudged me and I laughed, and we'd gone to bed after agreeing we were brothers more than friends, and *definitely* not lovers. I didn't tell him he was wrong about the bottoming thing, partly because I wasn't *solely* a bottom but mostly because of the dynamic.

Mario saved me. I'd never be able to be with him without feeling like I owed him, and I refused to owe anyone anything. I wouldn't have been able to live with that dynamic, and I think he knew that.

He knew me better than anyone, which is why he knew from the way I stiffened and the particular shade of red crawling up my neck that I was close to giving in to the part of me I tried so desperately to hide. His fingers tapped my knee lightly, comfortingly, just enough to keep me grounded so I could sip my water and take a breath.

"Okay, okay. I'm sorry. Tell us more about this dreamy nightmare," Breton said as I focused on cooling down.

"There's nothing else to say," I said. "He's going to be a pain to deal with."

"Yes, but *why*?" Pierre said exasperatedly. "What's wrong with Mr. Perfect Cheekbones?"

I clenched my jaw, thinking about Rick McDougall and his gorgeous blue eyes, his flaming red hair, and his exhausting mouth.

Exhausting in that he never shut up and was so full of himself that there had barely been room for me at that table.

"He's just... He's annoying," I said. "He spent half the meeting bragging about clubbing in Spain. He talks *so* much and says nothing. It's like pulling teeth to get him to focus, and when he does, he spouts off the most ridiculous... He has no idea what he's talking about, but he thinks he does."

"Does he actually have no idea, or are you just being a design snob?" Armand asked.

My jaw twitched. "Like... okay, for example. He's insisting on doing wood panels, but he wants chocolate mahogany."

Armand stared blankly at me and Breton glanced at Pierre, then back at me.

"And that's a problem because...?" Pierre asked.

"Mahogany is reddish-brown. Chocolate mahogany doesn't exist." I fidgeted with my napkin. "He doesn't want stained wood, and he doesn't care that mahogany darkens over time, and he doesn't care that what he *actually* wants is walnut or maybe teak. He wants dark brown mahogany with no reddish tones which doesn't fucking exist."

"So just tell him you'll do mahogany and use walnut instead," Breton said.

The stupidity was more than I could handle, and I stared at him, lips parted, before shaking my head. "Do you know how fast I'd be fired? I have some integrity, you know."

"Yeah, Breton," Pierre said in my defense, much to my surprise.

Then, less to my surprise, he continued.

"Sean can't lie or he'll have to answer to Mr. Jesus himself. It's one of the seven deadly commandments. 'Thou shalt not tell sexy men with fuck-me cheekbones that 'tis mahogany when 'tis actually walnut.'"

Armand and Breton howled as heat flared up my cheeks again. That time, no amount of gentle tapping from Mario could stop the darkness curling in my chest.

"Aw, don't go!" Breton whined as I shoved my chair away from the table and pulled out my wallet.

"I'm tired," I said stiffly. "One idiot was enough today. I don't have the patience to deal with you three, too."

Before any of them could respond, I threw some cash on the table and turned.

"Why do you have to antagonize him like that?" I heard Mario ask, his own chair scraping against the floor.

The three of them giggled like the children they were as Mario followed behind me.

"Don't blame me," Pierre called after us. "The devil made me do it. That means you have to forgive me, right, Seanie-bear?"

Three

I WAS CERTAIN THE devil made me.

Unlike Pierre, the devil didn't make me do *it*, whatever that inexplicit *it* was.

The devil just made me.

How else could I explain who I was? *What* I was? What kind of God would have made me, only to give me the life He had?

For a long time, I thought it was the opposite. I thought God had forgotten me, that He simply wasn't there, that it was nothing personal, since there were so many billions of other souls that needed His attention. What did He care for one gay kid from some nameless town in northern Manitoba? And that was okay. I mean, it wasn't *okay*, but I could *understand* that.

What I couldn't understand was why everything came crashing down at once. That was when I stopped thinking God had forgotten about me and started to wonder if He was punishing me.

The problem was, I didn't know what I was being punished for. I hadn't chosen to be gay.

Mario had said he realized he was gay when he was in elementary school. Armand figured it out in high school. I didn't know what Pierre's story was, but I knew Breton broke up with a girl because he realized he was more attracted to her brother than he was to her. I never had a moment like that; I never *realized* I was gay.

I just knew.

It was never even a question in my mind; when the adults at church used to joke about their sons and daughters getting married when they grew up, I knew I wanted to marry a boy. I never considered anything else. It had never been a choice. It had never even been something I didn't know.

It just was.

The problem with that, though, was that I didn't understand why it was always men-and-women. It was Adam and Eve, or Mom and Dad, or Joseph and Mary. And that confused me because I just was the way I was. I didn't understand why there was no Adam and Joseph or Mary and Eve. So, like any annoyingly precocious child, I asked.

Thankfully, I asked my mom.

It was a simple question, I thought. My sister, Lacey, was at a piano lesson and my mom and I were in the waiting room of the music school. Mom was sitting in a chair and reading a book while I was sitting on the ground using the table for homework when I looked up at her.

"Mom," I said.

"Hmm?" she asked distractedly.

"Why aren't there any families in the Bible with two men? Like, two dads? Or two moms?"

"Because it's a sin, honey."

The words rocked me. I stared at her, trying to process this complete bombshell of a revelation with my mouth half-open, as she kept looking at her book. My silence must have been alarming because her face changed suddenly and she looked up, her eyes wide.

"Sean?" she said.

"I was just asking," I said immediately.

She knew I wasn't just asking. The book was closed, she slipped off the chair and onto the ground beside me, kneeling as she put a hand on my shoulder.

"Don't let your father ever hear you ask that," she whispered, and then she pulled me to her chest and hugged me hard.

I might have been a kid, but I understood. And I understood that *she* understood. It wasn't something I could ask about or ever admit to. It was a sin. I'd been created a sinner; though it was something I couldn't control, I'd die a sinner.

I'd been made wrong.

The anger had started that day. I remember it as clearly as anything. My mom's arms were around me, my face pressed so tightly to her chest that I could almost feel her heart breaking because of me, and I realized I would never be able to tell anyone who I was.

What I was.

They still found out, of course. People, I mean. The kids at school knew I was gay as soon as they knew what the word meant. It would have been bad enough if it was just a normal small town with normal, terrible children, but it was more than that. Everyone in the town was religious in a vast, all-consuming way. It was a town where the church wasn't a *church* so much as it was an obsession. Where the "church" was less about worship and more about obedience and fear and power.

And I was the leader's son.

If God had made me, why did He make me like that? Why did He make an innocent child a sinner by nature and give that child to parents who would never, ever accept him? Why did He put me in a small town surrounded by children as indoctrinated as their parents before them in a church that celebrated hatred and brimstone over love and acceptance?

The answer was simple: He didn't. He hadn't made me in the first place.

Which meant the devil made me.

Four

"SEAN!" LEANNE WALKED PURPOSEFULLY to my desk as I put my work bag on my chair and shrugged my jacket off.

"Morning," I said cautiously. "What's wrong?"

"You're late for a client meeting."

My stomach dropped, and I lunged for my phone to check my schedule.

"What? No, I... I have no..." I pulled up my calendar, which was as blissfully blank as it had been when I last checked it. "I have nothing scheduled."

She raised an eyebrow. "So Mr. McDougall showed up for his next consultation meeting because he felt like it?"

"Next consultation?" I asked, confused. "But I just saw him a few days ago."

"He just scheduled a meeting for himself, then?"

I bit back what I wanted to say and started scrambling through my desk and bag for my notes on the Barker project. "Maybe. He seems a bit, uh, flighty."

"Hmm," she said. "That certainly explains why he's complaining about how early the meeting was scheduled and showed Monique a confirmation email with his appointment time."

I tried to swallow back my annoyance, but my mouth had gone dry. "Vincent didn't forward me the meeting invitation for this after I agreed to take the client on."

Leanne pressed her lips together. "I don't like hearing excuses or blame. It's your responsibility as the project lead to ensure you dot those Ts and cross those Is."

Not correcting her idiom almost killed me, but I held it in and nod obediently. "Right. I apologize."

"Make sure it's the last time you need to apologize," she said, turning on a heel. "Theo Barker is a *massive* client, and I was very hesitant when Vincent insisted you could manage it. Do *not* prove me right."

As she strode away, I caught sight of Vincent across the office. He grimaced and half-shrugged in some lackluster gesture of a plastic apology. I glared at him, then yanked my notebook out of my bag and took a half a second to longingly glance at my coffee cup. It wasn't worth Leanne's wrath to be even later, but starting the day with no coffee *and* having to meet with Rick McDougall again?

That was God punishing me for *something*.

"Man, I am sorry," Vincent said as I rushed by. "I'll forward the rest of the meetings I booked."

"How many fucking meetings did you book?" I grumbled.

"I managed to talk him down to once a week."

I told myself that if getting coffee wasn't worth getting on Leanne's extra-bad side, it definitely wasn't worth stopping to throttle Vincent for being a slimy, shady, absentminded snake of a human being. Still, the hand I had clenched around my notebook twitched, and I had to force myself to move forward without screaming at him. It took until I was nearly at the meeting room for the heat on my cheeks to fade and I took a breath before opening the door, hoping my skin wasn't flushed.

"There he is," Rick said brightly as I walked in. "Did you get lost on your way here?"

I smiled tightly as he laughed at his own joke, the corners of his eyes wrinkling as an unfairly gorgeous smile crossed his face.

"My apologies." I settled at the table across from him. "They didn't make me aware of the, uh, weekly meetings. This won't happen again."

"Darn." Rick picked up the extra-large coffee in front of him and took a sip. "I was enjoying the anticipation."

I wasn't sure if it was a joke, so half-laughed and opened my notebook. "So, uh, since the last time you were here, I've—"

"Hold up, hold up," Rick said lazily. He took another long sip of coffee. "How was your weekend?"

I stared at him, hoping I didn't look as unsettled as I felt. "Um, good, thanks. Yours?"

He shrugged one shoulder and twirled his coffee cup on the table. "It's been a while since I've been in one place for this long. I'm still getting used to it. And, I mean, last time I was on a break like this, my best friend *wasn't* planning a wedding to his lovely-but-insanely-busy-fiancée who apparently had to be coerced into attending a dessert tasting this weekend. Can you *imagine* not wanting to go to a dessert tasting?"

"Uh... not really."

He flipped his hand towards me. "Right? Obscene. So I was all alone all weekend. I went out to the bar, binged a show, went out again... you know."

I didn't know, but nodded anyway. "Right. Well, in terms of the floor plan for—"

"Where's your coffee?" he asked, ignoring me. "Are you one of those monsters that doesn't believe in our lord and saviour caffeine?"

I cleared my throat. "I'll have one after the meeting."

"Hmm." He took another long sip of coffee, then put the cup down on the table. "Would you mind grabbing one for me, actually? I can't function at a normal hour without coffee, let alone this ungodly time. Do people *honestly* work at..." He glanced at his phone. "... nine-fifteen? Ugh."

Of course he wanted me to fetch him a coffee. I felt my jaw clench and tried to smile again, though I wasn't sure if I was able to force my mouth into anything resembling happiness.

"How do you like it?" I asked.

"Rough, usually, but I'm known to enjoy a good cuddle now and then."

"You... what?" I asked, stunned.

Rick raised an eyebrow. "That was called a joke, Sean."

Half of me wanted to laugh. That half was further divided into wanting to laugh at the joke itself, wanting to laugh at the disbelief on Rick's face, or being forced to laugh at the sheer absurdity of a client I'd just met making *that* kind of joke.

The other half of me was the bubbling, burning anger that constantly lived in my chest, and that half of me stared at Rick blankly. That half was also divided further; part annoyance, part embarrassment, and part frustration.

All of me was lost in his stupid blue eyes as he held my gaze. It was only when one perfectly arched eyebrow twitched in concern that I cleared my throat and broke the spell.

"And your coffee?" I asked, not looking at him.

He paused for all of a second. "Surprise me. I haven't met a cup of coffee I didn't like."

I nodded and turned to the door, not realizing until the draft of air hit me how warm my face was. I let the door close behind me and pressed my fingers to my cheeks as I walked, hoping against hope that the redness I was sure was there would fade quickly.

What the hell had he been thinking, saying something like that? He didn't know me. He had no... but it *was* funny. If Mario had made that joke, I would have been on the ground laughing. Hell, if Pierre had made that joke, I would have been hard pressed not to laugh. But those were my... well, my friend and my friend's friend. Rick was a client. On top of that, a client I'd just met, and a client I wasn't exactly fond of.

He was also so, so beautiful, and the second he'd implied...

Well.

Joke or not, I couldn't help wondering how Rick liked it, and *that* thought was why my brain had stopped working and I hadn't been able to bring myself to even laugh awkwardly. The coolness of my fingers on my cheeks did nothing for the heat settled there, and I was so distracted that I nearly tripped over Leanne as I entered the break room.

"Did I not make myself clear?" she asked pointedly.

I cleared my throat, willing my heart to stop racing. "The client asked for a cup of coffee."

"Did he?"

"Yes," I said, grabbing a mug. "You can come ask him if you don't believe me."

She pursed her lips but said nothing. She didn't need to; the tension in the air told me everything about the relative thickness of the ice I was skating on. As efficiently as I could, I filled the mug and turned on my heel, nearly sloshing it from the cup as I hurried out of the room.

Rick was sitting where I'd left him, with one key difference: my notebook was no longer sitting unopened on the table, but was in front of him as he flipped through it.

"These are pretty good," he said idly, tapping on one of the absent-minded sketches I'd done of his boss's project. "I like this."

"Great." I tried to keep the aggravation out of my voice as I placed the mug on the table and reached across for my notebook. "Can I have that back, please?"

He flicked his eyes up, seemingly surprised. Apparently I hadn't done that good a job hiding how fucking inappropriate I thought it was for him to touch my notebook. For all of a second, his eyes met mine, though they clouded over as he glanced down slightly.

"Oh. Sure." His voice was toneless, like the colour and magic had been sucked out of it, and he looked back up as I grabbed my notebook.

It wasn't until I sat back in my chair that I felt the cool metal of my cross settle back against my skin. For the amount of trouble it caused me, I should have just stopped wearing the damn necklace, but I'd worn it my entire life. I felt naked without it. So of course, it had picked that moment to pop out of my collar, and of course that had been the moment he had glanced up at me, and of course that meant he thought I was a religious freak, just like everyone else did.

My stomach clenched, though whether it was from humiliation or anger, I wasn't certain.

"Your, uh, coffee," I said, not quite able to look at him.

"Oh, no thanks."

I looked up, startled. Rick leaned forward, long fingers pushing the mug across the table to me.

"I'm not done mine yet. You should drink that before it gets cold."

There was a wary look on his face as I took a moment to connect the dots and realize what he'd done.

"Oh," I said, and took the cup. "Uh, thank... thank you."

He smiled, but his eyes stayed cautious.

"Shall we get started, then? My boss wants me to attend another appointment after this, so I'd prefer not to run late."

His mood had swung so swiftly and completely that I could barely keep up, and the focus that had been absent at our last meeting was present in spades that day. The humour was gone from Rick's face as he listened to me talk about the design process and what I'd accomplished since our last meeting, which wasn't all that much since it had been just a few days earlier. He looked at the sketches in my notebook with a practiced neutrality, nodding as I presented solutions to the concerns he'd brought up last time.

As aggravating as he'd been during the first meeting, though, I couldn't say his complacent silence was any better. More than once, I glanced up, almost hopeful that he would say something funny again, but he didn't.

The emotion I felt about that confused me. I shouldn't have cared that much what Rick thought, but knowing he'd realized I was a freak, just like everyone eventually did, bothered me. I'd been dreading sitting through another meeting of him yammering and showboating, but now that he was quiet, I was almost... sad. I almost missed it.

"... which would solve the, uh, mahogany issue," I said a while later. "Chocolate mahogany just isn't a thing."

"Mmm," he said, nodding. "Sure."

I raised an eyebrow. "Yeah?"

He shrugged. "If you're saying it can't be done, I will pass that on to Theo. I doubt he'll have much of a concern."

"Right," I said. "Okay. Well, that about covers it for today."

He nodded brusquely and stood, picking up his now-empty cup of coffee. "Right. I'll see you next week, then."

"I'll ensure I don't get lost on the way," I tried to joke.

"Mmm," he said again, and I felt my skin turn warm again.

"I'll, uh, get the door," I said.

"We're not going to have a problem, are we?" he said just as I put my hand on the handle.

Frowning, I turned to him. "What?"

He folded his arms across his chest, the sleeves of his shirt tightening just enough to show a toned bicep that distracted me for a moment.

"Are we going to have a problem?" he repeated.

"I don't understand what you mean."

"Let me be clear, then. Are *you* going to have a problem with me?"

I was about to if he didn't explain what the hell he was talking about.

"Why would I have a problem with you?" I asked tiredly. "If this is because of my notebook, I'm sorry. I just didn't think it was appropriate to flip through my personal items when I was out of the room."

"Well, that's fair, but no," he said steadily. "But if the reason you've been so uptight around me is because I'm gay and you're religious, then you need to—"

I don't know if he finished his sentence. The laughter that burst out of me was so loud and so sudden that I shocked myself. I couldn't say if I was more shocked than Rick, though, whose eyes were wide and stunned as I leaned against the door, trying to catch my breath.

"What did—"

"I'm very, very gay," I said. "Trust me, the church hates me more than they'd hate you."

The wary expression on his face faded, replaced with a shadow of the jovial, arrogant asshole I had gotten used to over the course of the previous meeting.

"Well, that's a relief," he said. "I was almost devastated that my intuition about you was wrong, but it turns out you just have a horrid sense of humour. My joke earlier was *far* funnier than this is. Actually, that might be even worse than what I originally thought."

I shook my head, still grinning. "So you could work with me if I was a homophobe, but not if I don't laugh at your jokes?"

His legs were so long, he only needed to take a few steps to stride across the room, smirking as I opened the door.

"I'm glad you're learning," he said as he walked past me. "Now that I know you're capable of it, I expect a lot more laughter out of you when I see you next week, Mr. Lemieux."

Five

THE NEXT MEETING WENT horribly.

I mean, as far as the laughter quotient went, it went well. Despite my best efforts and annoyance at the fact that we were getting nothing done, Rick managed to make me laugh twice. However, it was a complete waste of time; all the progress we'd made when he thought I'd have a problem with his sexuality was for nothing.

"I'm fairly sure chocolate mahogany exists," he argued when I got him on topic.

"I can promise you, it doesn't. Not without a stain."

He pressed his lips together before parting them with a popping sound. "Maybe we need to rethink the wood panels."

I nodded, noted it, and promised a new set of drawings for the next meeting.

"Hmm," he said when he saw them the following week. "I like it, but now I'm not too sure about the second floor. The floor plan is just... meh."

"Meh?" I repeated, raising my eyebrows at him.

"It just needs some... you know." His teeth grazed his bottom lip as he studied the plans. "Like, maybe if..."

He said something, but I was so focused on the way he bit his lip that I didn't hear it.

"Does that make sense?" he finished.

"Yep," I lied, hoping he hadn't noticed the way I'd fixated on his mouth. "I can certainly rework it, but keep in mind that if you want to stay on schedule, we need to finalize the drawings next week."

Rick waved a hand at me casually. "Don't worry about the schedule. It's more important to have this house be absolutely perfect. I want a place Theo and Aspen can fill with babies one day. Or dogs. Either is fine."

I chuckled and he grinned.

"What about you?" he asked.

"What about me what?"

"Are you going to fill a house with kids one day?"

"Probably not," I muttered as I sketched a basic floor plan in my notebook. "I'm pretty sure I can't get pregnant."

It was his turn to laugh. "You know what I mean."

"I don't know. My sister was the one who wanted a brood of kids, not me." The words had left my mouth before I could stop myself.

I shouldn't have said anything.

Rick smiled. "Lots of nieces and nephews, then. That's way more fun. I don't have any siblings, but Theo... well, he doesn't have any munchkins yet, but his brother does."

My breath had frozen in my lungs, but he didn't seem to notice. There was a sharp prick of pain in my chest as I thought of Lacey and the fact that I'd probably never know if she had kids. I hadn't seen her for five years; when I'd left home, she was barely a teenager. Realistically, knowing my father and how the church pushed that kind of thing on people, she might be preparing for her own wedding already.

I wondered who she'd get stuck with in that little town. None of them deserved her. She was too sweet, too innocent, too... and I'd left her there with *them*. With *him*. And I'd never gone back for her.

I'd thought about it once or twice or a million times. I would daydream about it: going back to that fucking place, storming up to the house I'd left years earlier, and telling her to pack her bags. But reality always set in. I could barely take care of myself, let alone two people. And she'd only just turned eighteen; what I was considering before was literally kidnapping.

But she was eighteen now, and I'd held out hope for a while that she'd get in touch. My mom knew how to get in touch with me. But Lacey had clearly never asked how to reach me. And that meant that they'd got her, probably. She'd always been the good one out of the two of us. She would have wanted to do what she was told. So she...

She probably thought the same thing about me that the rest of them did. That I was broken. That I was wrong. And so I left her there. I never went back for her. I was the kind of weak person who couldn't bring myself to face my own personal version of Hell on the off-chance that I could save her when I didn't even know if she *wanted* to be saved.

The guilt of that consumed me.

"Are you okay?" Rick asked, his forehead wrinkling beneath his flaming hair as he looked at me with concern.

"Fine," I said, a little too quickly and a little too harshly. "The second floor, it's just... it'll take me a few days to get that redone."

He folded his arms and leaned back in his chair. "Nope."

"What?"

"That's a lie."

My stomach curled, tightening as a spike of anger threatened to jump into my chest. "Excuse me?"

He didn't seem to notice my struggle. "Tell me what's wrong."

"Nothing."

He sighed dramatically. "*Sean*, my darling—"

"I'm not your darling," I snapped. "And this is not your business."

There was a long moment of tension before I glanced up, certain my cheeks were red, and saw the disconcerted bemusement on his face.

"Right," he said. "My apologies."

"The second floor," I said, trying to push past the awkwardness. "Once you let me know how many bedrooms, we can finalize the drawings."

He was late for our next meeting. I tapped my pen against my notebook as I waited, torn between anger and embarrassment. The angry part of me was annoyed he was late; I *hated* when people weren't on time. The other part of me was worried I'd offended him when I told him to mind his business. I knew I'd been right to say it, but... well.

Slowly but surely, those weekly meetings with Rick were becoming a highlight, and I didn't know how to feel about that.

When he finally showed up a while later, I was both relieved and aggravated until I realized he was holding two coffees.

"You have to try this," he said, shoving one of them into my hands. "This place does an *amazing* latte."

"Thanks," I said, flushing a bit. "That was, uh, thoughtful."

He smiled at me, boyish playfulness drawn across his lips. "It's bribery."

"Oh, God, what now?"

He burst out laughing. "Don't hate me, but we want to add a pool."

"A *pool*? Where?"

He argued his point and waved it off when I said it would delay the project another week, plus add more construction time.

"Perfection is the aim, Sean, darling," he said. "Theo and Aspen won't mind waiting a little longer for their dream home. Plus, there's a bright side for you, too."

"Is there?"

He set those twinkling blue eyes on me, deep and clear and cold and inviting all at once. "Of course. It means an extra meeting with me."

"I thought you said it was a bright side," I said before I could stop myself.

He burst out laughing before I could panic about saying something so unprofessional to a client and raised his coffee towards me. "Good one."

The week after that, he wanted to add the wood panels back in.

"But regular mahogany is fine," he promised as I tried not to laugh. "Sean, did you hear me? I agreed to the mahogany."

"That... great," I said, shaking my head as I wrote it down.

"Take this as a moment of immense personal growth," he said flippantly, sipping his coffee. "That means we need to look at the studio again, though."

"What? Why?"

His head tilted back as he made a noise of disbelief that I knew was just his tendency to be overdramatic. While he pressed a hand to his chest theatrically, I tried not to think about how smooth the unblemished skin on his neck was as he bared it to me.

"Sean, darling, I thought you were supposed to understand design."

I flushed as he looked at me. "I do."

He pursed his lips playfully. "If we're using mahogany for the wood panels, the carpet in the studio is going to clash. I can't believe I have to explain this to you."

I had no idea what he was talking about; the studio didn't even *have* wood panels. "Right. Well, I suppose it's a matter of different tastes."

He crossed a leg over his knee. "Yes, and my taste is impeccable. Now, show me the pool so I can tell you how much I hate it."

"I don't think any of the original designs are even left," I complained to Mario that night when we went out for drinks.

"That doesn't bother you one bit," he said.

I frowned. "Of course it does. I've done all that work for—"

"—for the opportunity to see your sexy redheaded client week after week," he finished.

The waiter came up with a tray of drinks and set Mario's usual fruity concoction in front of him and a glass of wine in front of me.

"Oh, I didn't—" I started.

"I did," Mario said. "My treat. You deserve a glass of wine once in a while."

I shifted uncomfortably. "I'll pay for it."

"You will not," he said firmly. "Don't pull this 'too uncomfortable to accept gifts' thing with me. You know damn well I hate drinking alone."

"Well, I'll get it then."

He shook his head. "You also know damn well that I'm not letting you pay for a drink *I* ordered for you."

I stared at the glass of wine, then sighed and picked it up. Mario nudged me with his toe.

"Are you doing okay?"

"I'm fine."

"I know you're fine. I asked if you are *okay*."

"The bills are paid."

He sighed heavily. "Sean. You *know* what I'm asking."

I toyed with the stem of the wine glass. "I'm eating properly, I'm spending an appropriate amount on groceries, I've got the heat on when it's cold and the AC on when it's hot, and I'm not sitting in the dark at night because I don't want to run up the electric bill."

He studied me for a moment, then nodded when he saw I was telling the truth. "Next up, you need to start giving yourself an allowance to have fun."

I groaned. "Mario, I'm an adult. I can manage my own finances."

"Your idea of managing your finances is hoarding as much as you can in the bank and spending so little on your needs that you forget there's more to life than saving money and working." He looked at me pointedly. "I know why you do it. I'm not going to tell you that you shouldn't. I *am* going to remind you that you won't ever end up—"

"Don't," I said softly.

He stopped immediately, waiting a moment before reaching across the table and taking my hand. "You have a chosen family now."

I snorted. "I have you. Literally, one friend."

"Yeah, and then a bunch more who care for you even though they're idiots who don't show it very well and that you'll eventually realize are happy to have you around, even though you think they aren't. But also, I'm not going anywhere."

"As much as I appreciate knowing that, what brought this heartfelt moment of validation on?" I asked as he let go of my hand.

"Because you like this guy, and I think you should go after him. And I don't want to hear 'I don't have the money to take him on a date' as an excuse."

It was a testament to how well Mario knew me. If he'd made the same statement a week earlier, I would have spilled wine all over the table as I howled with laughter. A week before that, I might have dumped the wine on his shirt. That night, I stared into the glass, then watched the liquid ripple as I picked it up with a shaking hand and sipped it.

"I knew it," he said. "You should ask him out."

"He's a cl—"

"His boss is your client. Not him."

I cleared my throat. "I don't know hi—"

"You'll get to know him when you date him. That's what dating is for."

"He's probably not even into—"

"He brought you a coffee, makes you laugh, laughs at your jokes, and is pushing to get to know you better," Mario said boredly. "He's into you."

I glared at him. "Do you have an answer for everything?"

"No excuses, Seanie-bear. Ask your nightmare out to dinner or I'll come down there and do it myself."

"And what if he says no?"

Mario scoffed, fished the cherry out of his drink, and popped it in his mouth. "So what if he does? You move on."

So what if he does.

Six

MY FIRST LOVE WAS a boy named Jude.

My first kiss was a boy named Jude.

My first heartbreak was a boy named Jude.

He was a year ahead of me in school, but we were the same age. As a child, he'd been sick and his parents had pulled him out of school because they were constantly travelling back and forth to Winnipeg for treatments. He spent a ton of time in hospital beds, surrounded by doctors and nurses and stuffed animals while there were tubes up his nose and piercing his arms. If anything, he should have been held back a year, but Jude was *brilliant*. In that year he was out of school, he managed to get ahead of his class, and when he recovered and came back, the school skipped him ahead a grade.

The downside was that he was already smaller than the other kids in his grade and being sick left him even more frail. Everything about him was delicate, from his stature to skin that was so pale that inky lines of purple could be seen beneath the surface. His features stood out against that white skin: brilliant hazel eyes and blush pink lips and golden hair that seemed to shine.

He was beautiful, and I loved him; truly loved him, with every bit of me.

He was the only other gay person I knew growing up, and I only knew he was gay because he had gotten fed up with bullies calling him a fag one day and said, "So what if I am?"

So what if he was?

He found out "so what" immediately, when a boy named Aaron who had been teasing him gagged before shoving him.

"Don't touch me, fag!" he spat, despite the fact that he'd been the one with Jude in a headlock.

Someone aimed a kick at Jude's head. He rolled away but ended up curled in a ball around the foot of the person who decided to kick him in the stomach. I heard the breath go out from his lungs, then the sick, hungry sound of him trying to gasp for air, and part of me *broke*.

"Leave him alone!" I roared, rushing forward and pushing Aaron as he aimed another kick at the back of Jude's head.

"Oh good, here comes the *other* fag," said Simon, a gangly boy with beady eyes. "You queers are fucking disgusting, you know that?"

"Fuck you," I said seconds before Aaron's fist found my left cheek.

"You'd like that, wouldn't you?" he spat.

Simon grabbed my arms, and I wrenched myself away before managing to get a hit in of my own; he reeled away, his face turning as red as the blood that began dripping from his nose.

"Asshole," hissed Simon, and he shoved me to the ground.

I writhed and kicked, avoiding his feet and scrambling back onto my own.

"What's your dad gonna think, huh?" he taunted. "Gonna find out he's got a fag son, and then what? You think he'll shoot you and put you out of your misery right then 'n there, or's he gonna save you for Sunday so he can make an example of you, huh? Or's your dad queer just like you are, Sean?"

He hit me again and I hit him back. If there was one thing I was good at, it was fighting, and hitting, and dodging fists and feet. I could wriggle my way out of headlocks and had so far avoided broken bones or overly noticeable scars and bruises. By the time Simon and Aaron decided they were done with me, though, I had a black eye and split lip, and there was *no* way my parents weren't going to notice.

They stalked off some time later as I lay on the ground, trying to catch my breath. A few feet away, Jude was just sitting up; despite feeling like we'd been fighting for hours, he'd only just managed to recover from being winded, and I realized hardly any time had gone by.

"You okay?" I asked, my voice hoarse.

He cleared his throat, then crawled forward and collapsed right beside me. He seemed so *small*. I wanted to tuck myself around him, to be the shell that protected him from the world.

"Are you actually gay or do they just call you that?" he whispered.

I didn't say anything. I didn't even look at him. I sat completely still, as though that would stop people from being able to see me, breathing shallowly as I tried to keep my ribs from moving.

At least, I did until Jude's fingers brushed mine and I inhaled sharply. Slowly, I turned to see him looking at me, his eyes wide and vulnerable.

"So what if I am?" I whispered, and he broke into a smile.

"Then that'll be the best thing I've heard in my entire life," he replied, and his delicate fingers laced themselves between mine.

Seven

I DREAMED OF JUDE even while I was awake.

I dreamed of him when he was sitting next to me, imagining a world where I didn't have to stop myself from touching his hand or telling everyone how wonderful he was.

And he was. He was smart and funny and he loved hockey as much as I did. He had a mind that wandered in the most abstract of directions; there was nothing I loved quite as much as sitting with him while working on homework or studying the passages we were assigned at church, only for him to suddenly look up and say something mind boggling.

"Why is it okay for short people to ask tall people to get them something off a high shelf, but it's rude for tall people to ask short people to pick up something they dropped?"

"You know, technically aliens invaded the moon in 1969."

"Dogs can understand human words but humans can't understand dog barks, so does that mean dogs are smarter than us?"

"Why is it tuna fish but not chicken bird?"

Half the time, I'd burst out laughing and he'd grin as I shook my head and called him ridiculous.

The other half of the time, I would look at him incredulously until he turned towards me, his eyes big and innocent.

"What?" he'd say, and only then would I dissolve into laughter.

No one could know about us. People suspected, of course, and by suspected, I mean the kids who had always bullied us continued to bully us, so no one suspected that anything had changed. But I knew. *We* knew. We weren't alone.

He was the reason I left home, and the reason I left alone.

We got sloppy. Clandestine touches turned into bolder risks, and suddenly we weren't just grazing each other's fingers when we sat on the couch watching hockey or exchanging looks across the dining room table as we did homework. We had our first kiss behind the church after one Sunday service, just on the other side of the wall where his mother was asking my father for advice on what to do about Jude's strange behaviour. Muffled voices were the soundtrack to those first explorations, along with hearts racing so hard we could each feel the other's throbbing through his skin. Hands slipped beneath clothes, daring and eager and terrified as we touched each other in ways we knew would be condemned, as scared as we were emboldened to push things past feeling good to feeling *good*.

The first time I finished with Jude's hand over my mouth to muffle my cries, I was horrified. I had no idea how I was going to get home without anyone noticing, not just because of the wet spot on the front of my dress pants but because I was certain the guilt was written across my forehead. But I managed, and so did he, and things pushed further.

We stopped whispering sweet nothings to each other. Sweet nothings were reserved for scrawled notes that were tucked into a hymn book we passed back and forth, a silent protest against the things my father spewed from the front of the church. Each time he roared that the devil had claimed the souls of the homosexuals and the whores, of the sinners that apparently roamed everywhere but our little town, a thrilling shiver ran through my body because I knew. I *knew* that the service would finish and I would find Jude, and the sweet nothings we used to whisper would be replaced by three words murmured softly, passionately, and honestly.

"I love you."

"I need you."

"Kiss me again."

"Touch me there."

Each Sunday that passed was a Sunday closer to the day we could be together.

I dreamed of the day we would leave, of the day I would tell my father what I thought of him before taking Jude's hand and marching away to live my life. I dreamed that my mother would leave him, that she would take my sister and follow, and we would go somewhere else—anywhere else—and live happily without *him*.

That dream got me through everything. It got me through years of torment and loneliness and bullying. It got me through knowing I would never be accepted by my family. It got me through the day my father discovered us, through the moment my mother accidentally picked up *my* hymn book instead of *her* hymn book and saw the notes from Jude. It got me through her gasping and trying to hide the book a heartbeat too late, through the way my father twisted her wrist so hard I thought he was going to break it, through watching him stare at the page with a face as red as fire and as sour as brimstone.

It was all that kept me sane when Mom grabbed my arm after he walked away and said we had to go home right after the service. It was all I could picture as tears ran down my face while she raced across town in her old car, skidding on the ice and parking at an angle on the driveway as she ushered me and Lacey inside. I told myself again and again that it would be worth it as Lacey sobbed, so confused and so torn and so *young*, and I threw everything I could into a bag. The idea of a future with Jude was all I could hold on to when my father returned.

He hurled words at me that I'd heard a thousand times before and that hurt a million times worse coming from his mouth. Spit flew from his lips as he damned me, cursed me, belittled me. I was no longer his son, not that I ever truly had been; I was something blasphemous, something unholy, something perverted. I wasn't his child or God's child or the child of anyone but Satan.

He said he could save me. Not him personally, of course, but another preacher, one who had experience with saving people who suffered from "sexual brokenness." He knew the way to cure perversion, my father said, and I knew who he meant. I knew what his methods were. My father never questioned the fact that I had already looked into it; he never understood that I had spent my whole life wanting to be anything but what I was.

I knew who that man was, I knew what he did to people, and I knew it was quite the opposite of a "cure." I knew I'd kill myself before I let that man anywhere near my mind.

I told my father as much, and he said that might be for the best.

The house went silent when he did. I don't know why I fought him so long; I knew it wasn't worth trying to change his mind. Instead, I grabbed my bag, clung to my dream of Jude and the life I was sure we were going to have together, and walked outside.

It was painfully cold. I made it halfway down the block before slipping on a patch of ice and nearly crashing to the ground. My skin burned and then went numb, my nose dry and painful as clouds of breath puffed out of my mouth. I cried, sort of; the tears seemed to freeze in my eyes, clinging to my eyelashes and blurring my vision with crystals of salted pain. When I finally got to Jude's house on the other side of town, it took me two tries to hit the doorbell because my fingers were so stiff, and I was certain my lips were blue.

"Sean," he gasped when he answered. "What're you—"

"My dad knows," I whispered.

He went pale. "About me?"

I shook my head. "That I'm gay."

He nearly threw his neck out looking over his shoulder, then pushed forward and tucked the door half-shut behind him.

"My parents are home," he hissed. "You can't say that out loud."

"I need help," I said. "Please, Jude."

"I... uh," he said, shivering in the winter air. "I mean, what am I supposed to do?"

Maybe it was the cold, but my heart froze.

"D'you want... like, I have a bit of money, I guess?" he continued.

I stared at him blankly.

"What?" he asked after a moment.

There was no laughter that time.

"I can't, you know..." I said. "Like, I can't stay here for a day or two?"

"My parents will kill me. I mean, if your dad found out, he'd kick them out of the church."

My mouth twitched. "Come with me, then."

I didn't know what the look on his face was. Maybe it was regret. Maybe it was fear. Maybe it was discomfort. Whatever it was, it only meant one thing.

"I can't, Sean," he said. "I love you, but—"

But.

I turned around without saying anything.

"Wait." He grabbed my arm.

I swung around, shoved him away from me, and watched as he stumbled into the half-closed door.

"Don't," I said.

That day, my family was replaced by loneliness, my life was replaced by the unknown, and my dreams of Jude were replaced by cold, creeping anger that settled deep in my stomach.

So, as it stood, I suppose Mario had a point. If I asked out Rick McDougall—another man who was a dream, another man who could be a nightmare—and he said no, so what?

So *what*?

Eight

THERE WAS NOTHING IN the employee handbook about dating a client's personal assistant.

There wasn't a lot about dating clients, either. What was there was very clear: don't do it.

There *were* a lot of notes on how to define a client. A client, according to the handbook, was someone actively engaged in a project with our firm. Pre-existing personal relationships with clients weren't a problem, and personal relationships with clients *after* their projects were complete weren't a problem.

I wondered why that was so explicitly spelled out. Not because I didn't understand it, obviously, but because I wanted to know which higher-up had managed to sneak that phrasing into the handbook and who, exactly, they'd fucked.

I couldn't help it. I was curious, and gossip is always a little enticing.

Either way, the handbook was mostly useless. Rick wasn't a client, but he worked for a client. I took that to mean that asking Rick out would cross the line of what was appropriate, at least while we were still working on a project.

Of course, that didn't mean I couldn't work on getting to know him a little better. The only problem with that was I had next to no experience in trying to get to know *anyone* better. Breton hadn't been that far off when he asked if I was a virgin. I *wasn't*, but I'd also never had a boyfriend.

Jude didn't count. I might have loved him, but he wasn't my boyfriend.

I'd hooked up with more people than I'd dated, and I *had* dated, but I'd never gotten past a casual, disastrous second date. I hadn't had time. Leaving home at seventeen meant I had to grow up fast, and if it weren't for Mario, I wouldn't have made it.

I'd stumbled into his life by accident. Literally. I was at a club in Winnipeg and was half out of my mind when I tripped on something: possibly a foot or a discarded beer bottle, more likely just the air.

And Mario caught me.

And then I apologized and he laughed.

And then I laughed.

And then I puked on his shoes.

For some reason—and I don't know what that reason was, because if some drunk-ass kid had puked on my shoes, I probably would have punched them—Mario took me under his wing. He saw the brokenness in me. He saw what everyone else likely saw and refused to acknowledge; he saw how lost I was and how much I needed someone to just...

I just needed someone to help me.

I wouldn't have made it to Montreal if it weren't for him. I wouldn't have finished my high school diploma if he hadn't made me, which meant I would have never gotten into university. I would have never answered my mom's calls without him urging me to, which meant I'd have never found out that she'd taken my college fund out of the bank so my father couldn't touch it.

And if I hadn't found that out, I wouldn't have been able to finish university. I worked and applied for scholarships and loans and grants, but school was expensive. I lived with Mario for a while as he studied to be a hairdresser, but he had the luxury of knowing he had somewhere to go if he failed.

I didn't.

What that meant is he could party. He could bring home guys to fuck. He could go on dates or out to the club without the nagging, crippling angst buried in the back of his skull telling him that every dollar spent on beer was a dollar closer to not being able to pay my tuition. Every moment spent flirting with some drunk guy leaning against a sticky table in the club was a moment I could be studying, and what if that moment was the difference between passing and failing?

So I moved out, which was for the best, and focused on school while Mario tried to remind me that there was more to life than that.

But Mario had been right about Rick, as much as I hated to admit it. I liked Rick. I mean, he annoyed the shit out of me, but he made me laugh. He was thoughtful beneath the showboating and the sharp-tongued sass.

And he was just so...

It was unfair how gorgeous he was.

After my drink with Mario, I returned to the small studio apartment I'd called home since university. I tried with everything in me to think about anything besides Rick, but it was futile. His eyes invaded my mind; his hair glowed in my memory, catching light and throwing it, not like fire but like a prism, like he made light itself shatter and split into thousands of colours. His lips, his jaw, the freckle on his neck that I wanted to press my mouth against. The way he looked in his jeans, the way his clothing fit *so* right, the way he unsettled me and challenged me and drew laughter out of me like it was water from a tap.

I thought about him a lot that weekend. I did other things while I was thinking about him, things I'd steadfastly avoided doing while thinking of him, things that I couldn't deny myself of any longer. I wanted to know what his hands would feel like on my body. I wanted to know if he was truly joking when he said he liked it rough. I wanted to *taste* him so badly I could almost imagine it as I touched myself and wished it was him.

When my next meeting with Rick rolled around, I realized I should have spent more time figuring out how I was going to get to know him better and less time imagining him as I jacked off. This would have helped prevent the surge of guilt and embarrassment when he walked into the room smiling that damn smile and the awkwardness that hung heavy in the air as I tried to figure out how people *talked* to each other.

Instead, I stuttered my way through our conversation, barely able to look at him.

"You seem off today," he commented at one point. "Rough weekend?"

"Sort of," I mumbled, staring down at my notebook.

"Ahh," he said sagely, then snickered.

"What?" I asked, glancing up and frowning.

He looked somewhat guilty. "I just... never mind."

I put my pencil down and raised an eyebrow. "Tell me."

His tongue poked out briefly before he curled his lower lip into his mouth and I flushed, remembering how I'd pictured that *exact* action multiple times over the weekend. "I thought of something funny."

I rolled my eyes. "Are you going to tell me?"

"The last time I told you something like this, you turned so red I thought you might burst into flames."

There was a good chance I was about to do the same, though it was for a very different reason this time.

"Try me again," I said shakily.

Rick raised an eyebrow, studied me for a moment, then smirked. "I was going to ask you if it was the sad kind of rough or the fun kind of rough."

Sure enough, I turned red, but I didn't run out of the room that time. Instead, I chuckled and glanced down at my notebook.

"Not... no," I said. "Not the fun kind."

"Bad breakup or something?" he guessed.

I shook my head.

"Do you have a partner?" he asked haltingly. "Or..."

"No." Then, when he didn't say anything: "Do, uh... do you?"

"Nope," he said brightly. "Aspen used to ask me when I was going to settle down with a nice guy, but I kept worrying if I settled down, I'd miss the nice one, you know?"

I assumed he was asking me if I understood what he was trying to say, which seemed to be that he wasn't interested in settling down. I swallowed hard, reminded myself that I hadn't even asked him out so had no right to feel as dejected as I did, and picked up my pencil again.

"So the, uh, pool," I said. "Blue tiles or green?"

Rick looked like he wanted to say something, but something about the redness in my face or the panic in my eyes must have stopped him. "Green, I think. Theo would probably say blue, but he thinks everything should be blue."

"Does he?"

"It's his favourite colour." Rick leaned forward conspiratorially. "Between you and me, I think that's why he got together with his ex. Big blue eyes. But she was horrendous and thankfully he found his dear, sweet Aspen."

"She sounds lovely."

"Oh, she's horrendous too," he said. "But in the best possible way. One of the strongest women you'll ever meet. Scary, though. And stubborn as all fuck."

I raised an eyebrow. "I'm going to meet her?"

"Well, obviously," he scoffed. "She *is* your client."

I shrugged, trying not to smile. "I wouldn't know. I've dealt with you exclusively."

"That's because I have impeccable taste and they trust me implicitly."

"Is that usual for a, uh, personal assistant to do?" I asked, trying not to sound like I was talking down about his job.

Rick, thankfully, didn't take it that way. "Nope, but it falls more under my designation of 'official best friend.'"

I looked up, surprised. "Really?"

He pressed his lips together, playfully patronizing. "Well, *no*, I suppose it's not an official designation."

Shaking my head, I laughed. "No, I mean, you're best friends with your boss?"

"We were best friends before he was my boss. Theo and I grew up together. When he made it big and I had the choice to either hang out with him all the time or, like, get an actual job... well."

He gestured vaguely and grinned so brightly I couldn't help returning it.

"So you've known him your whole life then?"

"Fishing for all the deep, dirty details of Theo Barker's personal life?"

My face felt warm again. "No, I just—"

"Sean, darling," he interrupted. "I'm joking."

My mouth felt dry but I forced another chuckle. "Right."

Rick's tone softened, and he leaned back in his chair. "We've been friends since we were in diapers, literally. I think our parents must have realized before either of us could even talk that we'd end up being those outcast kids, so figured we should be friends."

"What do you mean, outcast?" I asked before I could stop myself.

He smiled. "You know what it's like. Kids are awful and it's about ten times worse when you're the gay kid."

I looked down at the table. "Yeah, I know."

"Theo had this horrible lisp growing up," he continued. "Like, *horrible*. The only reason I could understand him was because I listened to him learn to talk. It was like he was speaking another language, I swear. And I was the ugly loser with huge glasses and red hair who loved musicals."

I couldn't help it; I laughed. "There's no way *you* were ugly. Look at you."

The words were out of my mouth before I thought them; they were processing in Rick's ears before I even realized what I'd said. Alarmed, I stared straight down at my notebook as I felt his eyes on me. My shoulders tensed as I waited for the teasing and mocking I was sure was coming.

For some unknown reason, Rick took pity on me. "Getting rid of the glasses helped. First thing I did after Theo started paying me for being his best friend was get laser surgery. But, yeah. For most of our lives, it was just me and him. We had other friends, of course, but it was a small town so—"

"You grew up in a small town, too?" I asked, surprised.

"Yeah. You?"

I nodded. "Super small."

"Where? Maybe I've heard of it."

"There's no way," I laughed. "It was in northern Manitoba."

"Yeah, I don't know any towns up there. I grew up in Wakeham. In Ontario. Theo's parents and his brother still live there. Same with my parents."

"No siblings?" I asked.

"Besides Theo, a.k.a. the brother I never wanted." He grinned, folding one leg over the other. "It's kind of hilarious, since once in a while rumours will fly about the two of us, but he's about as straight as can be. Poor guy. But it's never been like that. I mean, he's attractive enough, but I never... you know? He's my friend."

I nodded, thinking of Mario.

"Anyway, my parents were old when they had me," he continued. "Tried for years, gave up on it, then bam, big ol' gay redheaded baby pops out, and I was so perfect they didn't bother trying ever again."

I wasn't quite sure how he did it. Suddenly, instead of me stammering and blushing, we were talking, and I was so entranced listening to the stories of his childhood and his family that I almost forgot to be nervous.

He told me about how his dad had just started using a wheelchair, joking about how unbearably optimistic and cheerful he was.

"Nothing gets him down," Rick said, shaking his head. "Last time I was there to visit, he wanted me to put flame stickers on it for him. I talked him down to racing stripes, at least."

His mother sounded like the kindest person in the world.

"Knew I was gay before I did," he laughed. "But it meant when I came out and the entire world seemed to turn against me, she was ready."

I thought of my mom and swallowed back a lump of emotion. "She sounds lovely."

I learned all sorts of things about Rick that day. He graduated high school but had never gone to university. He'd travelled the world with Theo, but never figured out where "home" was when he returned.

"Maybe Montreal," he said idly. "I mean, since Theo's going to be living here. I don't want to move back to Wakeham but I don't know many people here."

"You know me," I said without thinking.

Rick's eyebrow twitched and before I could even think of being embarrassed, his eyes had captured me.

"Do I?" he asked lightly. "I don't feel like I know much about you at all, Sean."

Before I could think of something—anything—to say, my phone buzzed on the table. I was thankful for the distraction for approximately two seconds before I saw what was on the screen.

"Oh, shit," I said, grabbing it.

"What's wrong?"

"Uh... nothing." I glanced down at my notebook. "It's, uh... we just, someone else needs the meeting room, and we didn't go over... well, anything."

My heart started to hammer. We were already weeks behind schedule because Rick kept changing his mind and I didn't have approval on any of the changes I'd made the previous week.

"Let's just have another meeting," Rick said. "My week's a little booked, but if you don't mind, we could schedule something in the evening? Talk about it over drinks?"

The hammering in my chest stopped. It was like my heart didn't know what to do; it froze, startled, stunned, disappointed and intrigued and... and terrified, which is what Rick saw flash across my face.

"Or I can schedule a regular meeting during working hours," he said gently.

I cleared my throat. "That would be best. We have a, uh, policy."

"Right. Of course." He stood, picked up his coffee cup, and started towards the door. "I'll book something at reception, okay?"

He was about to walk out. His hand was on the door handle and he was going to go into the hallway thinking I didn't want him. And that would be for the best, too, almost certainly it would be for the best. He was gorgeous and funny and smart but he was a distraction. He was a client. He was... he was...

"Rick," I said before he could open the door.

"Hmm?" came the response.

My fingers shook as I closed my notebook and I had to force myself to turn towards him.

"I can't go for drinks with you right now." I wished my voice would come out deeper, louder, stronger, but it didn't, and I swallowed hard. "But there's nothing wrong with seeing a former client. Like, after a project is done."

He stood still, not speaking, as my entire body seemed to tremble. When I finally looked up, his eyes were sparkling and there was a half-smile spread across his lips.

"Well, it's a good thing we'll be able to finalize everything at our next meeting," he said. "I'm putting my foot down, Sean, darling. No more of your unnecessary changes."

With that, he left the room. My breath returned and when I got back to my desk, I couldn't stop smiling.

Nine

"... SO SHE GOES 'I'm never coming back to this hellhouse of a coffee shop again.'" Pierre stopped and took a long sip of his drink for dramatic effect. "So I go, 'Ma'am, there's nothing you could have said that would make me happier.' And she gasps and goes 'well, I *never*,' and so of *course* I say—"

"'Well, I just did,'" I finished.

Pierre looked at me, a surprised laugh bursting out of his mouth. "Exactly."

I grinned and sipped my wine. "Nice."

Breton chuckled, shaking his head. "You're sure in a good mood today."

"Me?" I asked.

"Yes, you." Pierre leaned forward, the black eyeliner making the crinkles next to his eyes seem even more pronounced as a wily smile crossed his face. "What's got you all happy-go-lucky, Seanie-bear?"

I shrugged. "Just had a good day, I guess."

"You got laid, didn't you?" Armand said.

Breton howled with laughter. "Yeah, Sean. Something clearly crawled up your ass... or was it the other way around?"

They seemed more surprised than anyone when I laughed along with them.

"No, but seriously," Pierre said. "I've never seen you so... I dunno what the best word is. Relaxed? Open? Laid-back?"

Breton gasped. "It's the sexy redhead client, isn't it?"

I glanced at Mario, who looked amused as he idly toyed with the cherry stem.

"It is!" Armand said, delighted.

"Sean!" gasped Pierre. "You have to tell us *everything*!"

"There's nothing to tell," I said. "Nothing... nothing happened. Just something... I dunno. We talked a couple of days ago and we might go for a drink or something when the project's done."

I'd never quite believed Mario when he said that three others considered me a friend. I thought they put up with me because they liked Mario, since I only put up with them because I liked Mario. Still, it was hard not to feel like I'd been a little wrong as Breton squealed and Armand clapped a large hand on my shoulder. Pierre shifted in his seat, leaning in and demanding details about everything.

"I don't know when," I said for the zillionth time a while later. "When the project's over. He's not a client, but it's complicated because—"

"Wait, he's not?" Breton interrupted. "I thought—"

"His boss is my client. He's the personal assistant," I said.

"That's too bad," Pierre said. "I mean, don't get me wrong, he sounds lovely, but you know... it would've been lovelier if he were rich."

I rolled my eyes. "That doesn't matter to me."

"I *know*, but—"

"So who does he work for?" Armand asked interestedly.

I shook my head. "I can't—"

Pierre groaned dramatically. "Ugh, but *Sean*!"

"I have a confidentiality clause! I can't tell you who my client is."

"But he could, right?" Breton said.

"Who?" I asked.

"The sexy redhead."

I frowned, confused. "I mean, I guess—"

"Perfect," Armand said, grinning. "When you bring him to meet us, we're going to grill him so—"

Pierre interrupted him with a light smack on the arm. "Don't *tell* him that, otherwise he won't *bring* us the sexy redhead!"

Mario touched my knee as they bickered, his fingers tapping lightly. I looked at him, not sure why he was trying to ground me, only to realize he had a look on his face like...

If I didn't know better, I would have said it was pride.

"I told you so," he said as we left the bar later.

"What?"

He grinned. "The guys. I told you they like having you around and that you're one of us. You just needed to open up a bit."

I didn't respond and he looped his arm through mine.

"They're excited that you're happy. *I'm* excited that you're happy."

"Nothing's even happened yet," I said. "We just—"

"—agreed that you're interested in each other and want to get a drink together when you're done working together." Mario bumped his hip against mine. "That's something to be happy about."

I smiled, looking down at the sidewalk. "Yeah."

"When do you see him again?"

"Tomorrow," I said. "He's coming in for a meeting so we can finalize everything and then, God willing, we can get approval on the designs and move onto the next phase."

"I'll keep my fingers crossed for you," Mario promised.

My good mood had persisted for days after my last meeting with Rick and only increased after having drinks with my friends. I curled up to sleep that night with a smile on my face and butterflies in my stomach, feeling light and airy and happy in a way that was both foreign and addicting. When I woke early the next morning, I felt refreshed and excited.

Part of me was terrified at how giddy Rick made me feel. It felt unnatural to be so happy, but I couldn't help it. I liked him, and what was so bad about that? Didn't I deserve at least a bit of happiness? I mean, Mario was right. There *was* more to life than work and saving money and watching hockey. I'd worked hard to get to where I was. Maybe I didn't have to worry as much as I was.

Maybe it was time for me to feel safe.

I took my time getting ready for work, admonishing myself for panicking about what to wear. It wasn't a date; I'd been seeing him for weeks at that point and the clothes I'd worn to work hadn't failed me. Still, I stood in front of my wardrobe after showering, pursing my lips as I tried to pick something that looked nice without being obvious that I was trying.

At least my hair looked good. Mario had appointed himself in charge of my hair style, which was fine by me. Lately, he'd been leaning towards shortening the sides and leaving some of my curls longer on the top so they flopped onto my forehead. I ran the products he'd instructed me to use through my hair and let it dry while I ate breakfast, grabbed a coffee, and made my way to work.

My meetings with Rick were usually first thing in the morning, but since it was a make-up meeting of sorts, the only time we'd been able to get was just before lunch. That was fine; all it meant was that the morning passed like it was cold honey being poured out of a bottle.

I was in such a good mood that I didn't even mind how stupidly excited I was.

It wasn't until just before my meeting time that my mood faltered. I was filling out some mindless paperwork when Monique, the receptionist, shot through the office with a squeal of excitement trailing behind her.

"Sean! You could have warned me!" she squeaked as she reached my desk.

I frowned. "What?"

"That *Theo Barker* was coming in today!" she hissed, but her face was bright and flushed. "Oh my God, I'm such a huge fan, and all of the sudden he's just walking in the office and I had to sit there pretending like I wasn't literally *just* listening to his last album and—"

"Wait, wait," I said. "Theo Barker is here?"

"Yes, for your meeting," she said. "I said you'd be there in a minute, but he said no rush. And I think Leanne popped in to say hello. I mean, he's a *massive* client."

Right. Like I wasn't about to rush to the meeting room to find out why the hell Theo Barker had shown up unannounced when I was expecting Rick. The light, airy feeling I'd been basking in since last seeing him crashed around me, replaced with the cold weight of the cautious anxiety I was used to.

"Thanks, Monique," I muttered, grabbing my notebook and standing up. "I'll head there now."

"Ask him if he'll sign something for me!" she teased.

I ignored her, dread settling in my stomach. By the time I reached the meeting room, I was surprised there wasn't a literal cloud over my head.

The door was ajar and I could hear voices spilling out, but couldn't quite make out what they were saying.

Taking a breath, I pushed the door open and stepped in.

The room was crowded. At least, it was comparatively crowded. Normally, I sat on the side of the table near the door while Rick sat across from me. My usual spot was still open, but across from the empty seat was Theo Barker.

I knew him, of course. Everyone did. His tanned face and warm brown eyes were on the covers of magazines and all over the internet. I enjoyed his music, mainly because I didn't listen to the radio and so didn't hear the same songs on repeat all the time. I was somewhat surprised as he looked up; I'd expected someone... I wasn't sure. More intimidating, I suppose. As it stood, there was an air of stylish disheveledness around him. He had thick, longish hair that seemed naturally messy and wore a clean but comfortable looking hoodie. There was a laid-back casualness about him as his eyes met mine and for half a second, I thought things might be okay.

Then I looked to his right.

The woman sitting there was incredibly beautiful, her face unblemished and her eyebrows impeccably groomed. Her hair was wildly curly, but pulled back into a tidy bun. As disheveled as Theo Barker was, she was put together in a white blouse and grey blazer. She looked up as soon as the door was open, staring at me with such severity that I stopped in my tracks.

Aspen, I assumed.

On the other side of Theo sat Rick. I didn't look at him.

"Sean," Leanne said from her spot at the head of the table. "I hope you don't mind, but I'd like to sit in on your meeting with Mr. Barker."

"I don't mind at all," I said cautiously. "Good morning, everyone."

"Morning," Theo replied. He stood and extended his hand across the table. "Call me Theo, please. Nice to meet you."

"And you," I said, shaking his hand.

He smiled warmly, then gestured to the woman beside him. "This is Aspen, my fiancée."

"Pleasure," she said, her tone indicating it was anything but.

"Sean Lemieux." My voice threatened to crack, but I managed to keep it steady. "My apologies. I didn't know we were all meeting today."

"It was a last-minute decision," Theo said. "Rick mentioned we'd be finalizing some stuff today, so we figured we should be there for some of that."

"Of course," I said. "Great idea."

"Mm-hmm," said Leanne. "Why don't we get started?"

I sat down, well aware of the four sets of eyes on me as I opened my notebook and pulled out the last set of drawings I'd done. My mouth was dry and I kicked myself for subconsciously assuming Rick would have brought a coffee for me.

I wasn't entitled to a coffee from him and he wasn't obligated to bring one, but he'd gotten me into the habit of expecting it.

"Right," I said. "So, why don't we do a whole overview of the designs and then I'll get into the changes we need to finalize from our last, uh... last few meetings."

It couldn't have gone worse if I'd tried.

"Wait, one sec," Theo said as I started talking them through the first drawing. "I thought... can I see that?"

"Of course," I said, passing him the drawing and trying not to puke as he stared at it, frowning. "Is there a problem?"

"I just thought we had said..." He shook his head. "Maybe I'm misremembering. It's fine."

It wasn't fine, though.

"Really?" he said when he saw the studio.

"What's wrong with it?" Rick asked haughtily, though I still didn't look at him.

Theo twisted his mouth to the side. "I mean, the carpet is just... that's not what I was expecting."

He raised his eyebrows at the wood panels. "I was hoping for something less reddish. Is there a reason it has to be mahogany?"

"There are *how* many bedrooms on the second floor?" He didn't ask before taking the drawing that time.

Then, the crowning glory: "Wait, what do you mean, the *pool*? Since when do we have a pool?"

Until that point, Leanne had been silent.

"This is unacceptable," she said before I could respond. "Sean, could you please explain to me why the client is unaware of the *massive* changes you've made to their design? Where is the original consult sheet?"

"I... here," I said thinly, pushing it towards her. "The changes were—"

"Is this why the construction's been delayed so much?" Aspen interrupted. "I was under the impression it should be well under way by now."

"It should be," Theo said, though he looked at me apologetically. "I just don't understand—"

"I think it's clear," Aspen said, and those terrifyingly harsh eyes bored into mine again. "How much extra were you hoping we'd pay for this?"

"That wasn't—"

"Mr. Barker, Ms. Haws, I'm so sorry," Leanne said. She reached across the table and grabbed the rest of the papers I had spread out. "We clearly made an error of judgement here. I take full responsibility, of course; I should have been watching Sean's work much more closely. Sean, I'm not sure why you felt the need to keep this from me, but I had no idea that none of these changes had been approved."

"But they were!" I tried to hide it, but the desperation in my voice was so obvious that Theo winced. "I've been meeting with Rick weekly and—"

"There is no reason for a client to be unaware when you are making *huge* changes to the initial design! Mr. Barker was very clear in his initial meeting—"

"I wasn't at the initial meeting!" I said. "Vincent was supposed to—"

"Enough with your excuses!" she hissed.

"They aren't excuses."

The deep voice resonated throughout the room, strong and obstinate. I still couldn't bring myself to look at the source of it, instead staring down at my notebook.

"Mr. McDougall, with all due respect—"

"Some respect is due to Sean," he said pointedly. "I made those changes. I've been meeting with Sean on Theo and Aspen's behalf and approved all of this."

"You *what*?" Aspen said sharply.

"Aspen, I'm sorry. I didn't realize you were so upset about the delays," Rick said. "But this is on me. I asked for and approved every single one of these changes. Sean did exactly what I asked and was more than accommodating."

There was a beat of silence, then Theo laughed and Aspen sat back in her chair, the expression on her face somewhere between annoyed and exasperated.

"Asshole." Theo shook his head as he grinned at Rick.

"I was trying to help!" Rick said, then looked at Leanne. "None of this falls on Sean. I'm responsible for the delays."

Leanne's expression didn't change. "Be that as it may, it's Sean's responsibility as the project lead to ensure he's communicating with everyone involved. Regardless of who's to blame for the delays, this is not the kind of service we offer our clientele."

My stomach dropped. I felt Rick's eyes on me but didn't look at him. Leanne kept her eyes on me, her face like stone.

"Do you have any additional notes or information on this project that we haven't seen?"

My throat was so dry it ached. I knew what she was about to say. "There's some in here." I pushed my notebook towards her.

She took it, glancing down at the page. "I'll return this after the meeting. As of now, I'm taking over this project."

"I don't think that's—" Rick started.

"We'll discuss this internally later," Leanne continued, ignoring him. "Ask Monique to schedule a one-on-one for us immediately after lunch."

I nodded mutely. With every ounce of strength I had, I stood up, keeping my shoulders square and my chin up. Leanne was hurriedly reading my scrawled notes, but I felt three sets of eyes on me. I didn't look at any of them as I turned, trying to hold the final shreds of my dignity in place as I left the room.

Ten

I MANAGED TO KEEP my face neutral as I grabbed my wallet from my desk and went to reception. My voice didn't falter as I asked Monique to book my one-on-one, even though she stared up at me with a look of horrified confusion on her face.

"What happened?" she asked.

"Nothing."

"But—"

"I'm taking an early lunch."

Before she even realized what was happening, I was out the front door. There was no conscious decision on direction; my legs simply started moving, carrying me away from the office as fast as they could without full-on running.

It wasn't until I was halfway down the block that the facade of confidence and self-respect broke. I felt it happen; my heart threw itself against my ribs and fury flooded my veins. There were blessedly few people on the sidewalks, being still far too early for lunch, so no one saw the redness of my cheeks or the boiling tears gathering in my eyes. I walked quickly, so fast and purposeful that my hair bounced on my forehead and the air felt like cool pin pricks on my skin.

Part of me was screaming to call Mario. I *needed* Mario. I needed to be grounded, I needed someone to tell me it was okay, I needed to scream and cry and lash out to someone who would understand and not judge and he was the *only* person I could do that with. I knew that as much as I knew anything, but I couldn't call him. My hands were shaking, and I seemed physically incapable of unclenching my fists. The angry part of me was so riled up, so thoroughly furious, that I doubted I could have even formed words.

Instead, I walked, purposeful strides that did nothing to satisfy the roiling energy begging to be let out of me. The muscles in my arms tightened and loosened, aching to be used, aching for someone or something to strike.

I was not in control.

It was the worst possible state to be in when I heard my name being called from behind me. I didn't know how many times he said my name before I recognized it for what it was, but by the time I realized it was him, it was too late for me to escape.

"Sean, *wait!*" he called.

I didn't. I forced myself to turn off the main street and down a quiet side street, my heart fighting the physical limitations of my chest cavity.

"Sean, for God's sake!"

For someone with such long legs, he sure was having a hard time keeping up with me.

He caught up a few moments later by jogging, gentle panting the only indication that he was mildly out of breath. I didn't look at him. I couldn't look at him. It took everything in me, every sane bit of me that was left beneath the demon that was taking over my senses and emotions and actions, to keep my eyes forward. It was his fault, entirely his fault, but I couldn't... I didn't want him to see that, I didn't want him to see the stinging tears in my eyes, I didn't want to yell or scream or worse. But I was so *mad*. And I couldn't control it, and he was there, and I... I was about to lose everything.

I couldn't look at him. I focused on the end of the block, staring straight ahead, knowing if I looked at him, I'd snap, and if I snapped, I'd—

"Sean, please." He grabbed my arm and using it as leverage to pull himself in front of me.

If he thought I was going to stop, he was wrong. I ran into him, dipping my shoulder to nudge him out of the way as I passed. He stumbled, a surprised grunt the only noise he made, and then I was alone.

Well, I was alone for a moment. The persistent fucker just didn't want to give up.

"For fuck's sake!" he said from behind me, then grabbed my arm again. This time, he held on, forcing me to face him. "I'm trying to apologize!"

I looked up into blue eyes the colour of a winter sky on a sunny day and I broke, shattering like ice on a lake.

And he saw it, too. Just a moment too late.

"I don't give a fuck!" I wrenched my arm away from him. "Your apology is bullshit, Rick."

He looked affronted. "I'm *sorry*, I didn't think that—"

"You didn't think? What a fucking surprise. Are you even capable of thinking?" I laughed, the sound high-pitched. "You have no idea, do you? You've never had a fucking job that wasn't just hanging out with your best friend all day, every day. You have no concept of what it's like to actually *work* for a living and all the shit that goes into keeping a job like a fucking adult, do you?"

A muscle in his jaw twitched. "Okay, I deserved that, but—"

"But nothing." I blinked hard, but despite my best efforts, a scalding tear burned a trail down my cheek. "You decided to play some fucking game with my life and now I'm going to lose my job and I'm going to, I'm going... I'm going to—"

"You're not going to lose your job," he said fiercely. "I won't let that happen."

"You don't just get to decide that!" My voice came out hoarse as I forced it past the tightness in my throat. "Leanne's not going to give a shit what you say, she's only going to see that I fucked up and then she's going to fire me and I'm... you have *no* fucking idea, with your goddamn perfect family and friends and your fairytale fucking life."

I couldn't name the look on Rick's face. Disgust, maybe. Horror, revulsion, embarrassment on my behalf. Pity. Torment. Shame. Desperation.

Regret, maybe.

It didn't matter.

"Please take a breath and just... you're upset." If he thought the softness of his voice was soothing, he was wrong. All it did was make my skin burn warmer, flaring as he talked down to me like I was a child or a particularly ill-tempered horse. "You have every right to be but I want to help, okay?"

"You've done enough," I spat.

"Sean, please." He looked pained. "I just wanted—"

"Wanted what?" Anger surged through me, taking over any rational thought and turning me from human to the collection of transgressions I was. "Wanted to fuck with me? Ha-fucking-ha, Rick." I took a step closer to him, chin jutted out as my body threw out flight and switched to fight. "What'd I do to you, huh? You were bored? You're just a bully?"

"I'm not—"

I stepped closer still, craning my neck up so I was as in-his-face as I could get considering the inches he had on me. He stood firm, unblinking as I drew myself up.

"You fucked up my life, I'm going to lose my job and my paycheck and I'm gonna lose everything again. Is that enough for you or do you want more?"

"Wait—"

"Here you go, then," I said, ignoring him. "Stop with your goddamn mind games and just do what you fucking wanted to do."

"I'm not going to fight—"

I shoved him.

He kissed me.

He'd been ready, somehow, for me to try to push him away. He hadn't budged an inch; he simply grabbed my biceps and dipped his head, and suddenly the trails of wetness on my flaming cheeks were pressed against comparatively cool skin, my breath captured by the soft mouth claiming mine. I froze, eyes open, as stunned as I was exhilarated, the devil inside me silenced as my body melted.

I closed my eyes.

If life was a fairytale, that would have been the part where I learned to believe in magic. I would have said the anger evaporated from my body as his breath caressed my skin. One hand left my bicep and moved up to my cheek, his fingers dancing against my jaw before gently deepening the kiss. If life was a movie, I would have clutched at him, surrendering to the blaze of emotions catching throughout my body.

And for a moment, it was. For a moment, the world froze and all that mattered was the electricity that surged through my body. For that beautiful, amazing, heartbreaking moment, I kissed him back and let him feel the need and desperation and desire that bubbled and churned and boiled over. I touched him. I revelled in him. I let myself taste him the way I'd wanted to so badly taste him before... before. I let him kiss me with a passion I'd never known and a heat I only associated with anger, and pain, and hurt.

Life wasn't like that, though. It wasn't a movie, and it wasn't a fairytale, and Rick McDougall wasn't a knight in shining fucking armour. Rick was about to be my downfall, and even though his mouth was soft and inviting and comforting, it couldn't distract the anger in me for much longer than a heartbeat.

I pushed on his chest again, though it had about as much an effect as pushing on a brick wall. It made him hesitate, though, and I wrenched my head away from his. He let go, stepping back and holding both his hands as though to calm me.

"Sean—"

"No," I said. "*No.*"

"I'm sorry."

"I don't give a shit." My voice cracked and I pushed a hand across my cheek, suddenly humiliated by the moisture there. "This might be a game to you but it's not to me."

"It's not a game!" he protested. "I get it, you're pissed, and you should be, but I fucking swear to God this isn't a game."

Of course he'd swear to God.

"I'm done," I said. "This is my fucking life and it's all I had."

"You still *have* it," he said.

But I'd already started walking away, and this time, he didn't follow.

Eleven

After anger comes shame.

It was a state I was used to. Shame, I mean. Shame was my default. Shame was how I'd grown up and what I'd been taught to feel about myself. It was shameful to be who I was. It was shameful to sin. At its core, it was simply shameful to be human, really.

But shame after anger was a different kind of shame. It wasn't shame for how I'd acted, but how I'd *reacted*. I should have been more ashamed about getting in Rick's face and basically screaming at him to fight me like I was some kind of beefed-up aggressor dripping with toxic masculinity, but I wasn't.

I was ashamed of the redness of my face and the tears in my eyes. The fact that he'd seen me in pain, that he'd heard my voice crack, that he'd felt my hands shake when I shoved him and my indulgent sigh when he kissed me... that was what I was ashamed of.

Something in me knew that wasn't right. The other part of me figured I was broken anyway, so it didn't matter.

I walked for a while, wandering purposefully down streets and blocks, letting the surges of anger and pain flow off of me until I could breathe without my heart knocking against my ribs. By the time my pulse steadied and my anger was tucked back into the place I always kept it, it was after the proper lunch hour had started. I ducked into a cafe, ignoring the curious glances from the people in the lineup as I made my way to the washroom. There, I ran the tap until the water was as cold as it would go and splashed it on my face. There was nothing I could do but wait for the red surrounding my pupils to fade, but the coolness of the water calmed the pink flush on my face and the swollen puffs of skin around my eyes and cheekbones. Carefully, I wetted my fingers and ran them through my hair, tidying the curls that had started to frizz up while I wandered.

Then, I walked back to the office.

It was mostly deserted. The reception desk was manned by a bored-looking intern whose name I couldn't remember and who didn't look up from her phone as I walked by. Nerves tightened in my stomach as I glanced habitually towards the meeting room, but the door was open. Aspen, Theo, and Rick were all long gone.

I spent the rest of the lunch hour at my desk in the quiet office, subtly going through my drawers and putting any personal items into my work bag. In my time at the firm, I knew of three people who had been let go, and not one of them had returned to their desk after meeting with Leanne. Monique usually came by the next morning and went through everything, packing up any personal items into boxes that got shipped to the former employee.

I didn't want her going through my stuff in front of everyone, even though aside from my coffee mug, a novelty pen Mario had given me, and a few sundry things like mints and aspirin, there wasn't much of note.

Well, except for the picture.

I didn't keep it pinned to my cubicle wall like everyone else did. The picture was tucked in my desk drawer. Looking at it didn't make me happy; I had no idea why I even bothered keeping it. Maybe because it was the one of the few connections I had left.

Habitually, I put my thumb over my father's face. I couldn't bring myself to scratch it out and the way he was posed, I couldn't cut him out of it without trimming part of my sister's head. Considering Lacey was the only one in the photo I didn't feel anger for—guilt, yes, all-encompassing guilt, but not anger—I didn't want to ruin it.

We were just kids in the picture, maybe six and ten. We had on horrible matching sweaters and each of us had a gold cross conspicuously displayed over the collar. Lacey had her tongue sticking out and her eyes crossed, and my teeth were over my upper lip as I looked at the camera with wide eyes. Behind us, our parents had no idea that the professional photo was being taken less-than-seriously, and it was only after my mom saw the proofs that they realized it. She'd loved it, though, and I'd never forget the way she tossed her head back and nearly cried with laughter when she saw it.

I didn't have a lot of memories of my mom smiling and laughing like that.

She ordered plenty of that particular image, much to my father's dismay. He refused to display it on the wall like our other family photos, but my mom had always kept a small copy of it under a magnet on the fridge.

Just before leaving home for the last time, I'd snatched it off the fridge, the magnet going clattering across the linoleum. It was the only picture I had of them.

That didn't go in my work bag. I tucked it into my wallet, sandwiching it between the smooth side of two cards before making sure it wouldn't get creased when I closed it.

Then, it was time.

People flooded back into the office. I had no idea if they knew about the shitshow that had happened just before lunch and I didn't care. If I got strange looks or pitied whispers, I didn't notice.

Leanne's office was down a separate hallway from the general office area. It sat in the corner of the building, of course, and had large windows with curtains she kept drawn almost all the time. I'd only been there a handful of times before; when I'd been hired, when I'd been promoted from probationary to full employee, when I'd been admonished for two of the three projects Vincent had thrust on me unexpectedly, and now, to be fired.

The door was open when I approached. Monique was standing in the frame, making notes as Leanne talked to her, but turned her head when she saw me.

"Hi, Sean," she said, her voice falsely bright.

Leanne went quiet for a moment. "We'll pick this up later, Monique. Please head back to your desk."

She nodded, then looked up with wide eyes as she walked past me. "Good luck."

I nodded once, then walked into Leanne's office. I stopped just inside the door, something rooted deep inside me telling me I had to wait for permission before I sat down.

She was sitting behind her desk, my notebook and drawings from the Barker project in front of her. It wasn't until I had been standing there for a long, awkward moment that she looked up from them and folded her hands.

"Sean." Her face was unreadable. "Close the door, please."

I started to turn instinctively, then stopped and frowned. "It's just us?"

Leanne raised an eyebrow. "Who else did you expect?"

My face felt warm. "I thought HR might be here."

"Do you feel like you need a representative?" she asked, her face still neutral. "I can have someone come by."

I considered it for half a second before shaking my head and closing the door. I just wanted to get it over with.

"Have a seat." She gestured at the chairs in front of her desk.

I did as I was told, and then the games started again. She didn't speak for a moment, instead looking back down at the drawings. I watched silently as she put on a show, flipping through the pile and studying each drawing in turn.

"These are very good," she said.

"Thanks," I said flatly.

She glanced up at me. "You're how old?"

"Twenty-two."

"And you've been here for..." She glanced at her computer screen. "... not quite a year?"

I nodded, and she sighed.

"This is not the level I expect from someone in your position," she said.

My jaw twitched as I clenched it *hard*, trying with everything in me to keep my mouth shut.

"These are higher quality than many of our senior team members, let alone someone in the first year of their career." She put the drawings in a stack and folded her hands on top of them. "You have natural talent,

Sean. And don't think that I don't notice you working harder than anyone else. Those two things combined will get you far. But..."

But.

"They won't get you everywhere. Client management is a massive part of this role and your lack of people skills is holding you back."

And there it was.

"I understand," I said.

"This type of client should have never been assigned to you," she said bluntly. "That was an oversight on my part. I spoke with Vincent at the time and I will be speaking with him again."

I didn't know why it mattered for her to tell me that, but I nodded anyway.

"There are a lot of subtleties to a project like this," she continued. "And I wouldn't expect someone of your experience level to have those skills. That is something developed after years of working with clients. To be frank, however, you are below my expectations for *any* staff member at this firm for client relations."

She paused, staring at me until she was sure I understood her words. I did, of course, and I stared back, determined to keep looking at her until she said what she needed to say. She held my gaze and I assumed she was waiting for me to look away, to fall, to turn red with embarrassment or apologize for being terrible at dealing with people like people weren't terrible to begin with.

I refused to look away. I was *going* to face this head on. I was *going* to take it with grace and strength.

"Client relationships are a cornerstone of our business," she said. "It's what sets us apart from our competitors and why we have a client retention rate far higher than most in our industry. To work here, Sean, you need to have an intrinsic understanding of that."

I nodded again.

"So, starting Monday, you will be attending a mandatory client satisfaction seminar twice a week. The entirety of the course lasts six weeks, at which time we will—"

"What?" I said before she finished.

Leanne looked taken aback. "Excuse me?"

"Wh... why?" I asked, flabbergasted.

Pinkish splotches appeared on her cheeks. "I *just* said that client relationships—"

"No, I mean—" I stopped, sitting back in my chair and frowning. "I thought I was getting fired."

Leanne was not the kind of woman who liked to be interrupted. I mean, no one likes to be interrupted, but Leanne was not the kind of woman that people interrupted and walked away unscathed. She didn't tolerate stupidity and had expectations that were next to impossible to reach; impressing her just meant she wasn't as disappointed in you as she was in everybody else. There was no pity with her, no mercy, no exceptions.

She was the kind of person who I thought would fire me for interrupting her because I was confused about not being fired, but as it turned out, she wasn't.

Her response wasn't immediate; she let my words hang for a moment, tilting her head to the left. Then, her face softened—as much as something made of rock can soften, anyway—and she took a breath.

"No. You will be attending this seminar, after which you will report back to me about what you've learned. You will not be handling any new clients on your own; I will be pairing you with different senior team members to shadow and learn their processes, which is something I should have been doing in the first place. Save for the Barker project, which you will be finishing up as lead—"

"*What?*" I said before I could stop myself.

Leanne looked annoyed. "Sean—"

"Sorry." The strength and grace I'd been hoping for failed me and my voice cracked.

She took a breath and let it out. "Mr. Barker stated he would drop the project entirely if you were removed from it. Mr. McDougall maintains that the delays were his fault and was insistent that your work was exemplary. By my review, he's correct." She pushed my notebook across the desk. "Mr. Barker and Ms. Haws had notes about what changes they would like to see made and what they would like to maintain. I have recorded those changes for you to make before the next meeting. Mr. McDougall will attend as scheduled with the understanding that he is *only* to make minor changes and approvals."

She went over a few more probationary measures I had to follow: she'd be personally reviewing my notes and drawings after the meeting. I was to give her a report of what I learned at the client relations seminar. I was to sit in on her client meetings in the secretarial role Monique usually filled so I could be exposed to how she personally handled clients.

When all was said and done, I wasn't fired. I wasn't even demoted. Astonishingly, I was being set up for a promotion, of all things, with Leanne herself mentoring me.

"Any questions?" she said.

I shook my head, staring at the top of her desk as I tried to process everything she'd said.

"Good. Get back to work." She tilted her head towards my notebook. "There were a *lot* of changes."

I recognized the dismissal and stood up, collecting the drawings and my notebook.

"One more thing, Sean," she said as I turned to leave. "I apologize for my reaction in the meeting."

I blinked twice as Leanne looked at me steadily.

"You were given an extensive project without the support you needed. You produced incredible work and handled a difficult client to the best of your ability. I did not give you the opportunity to explain what happened and handled things poorly myself." She cleared her throat. "I understand Mr. McDougall enjoyed working with you very much. I appreciate that despite a need for further client service training, you maintained a positive working relationship with him. So, I apologize."

"That's... thank you. I, uh... apology accepted." I cleared my throat. "I apologize for... well."

"Accepted," she said shortly. "You were put in an awkward position. I hope this arrangement will help make up for that."

I still hadn't entirely processed what had happened after walking to my desk. I felt exhausted, unsettled, and relieved all at once. I didn't know how I managed to get out of her office with my job intact.

That was a lie. I did. Rick must have gone back to the office after he... after I pushed him. Theo Barker would have no reason to insist I stay on his project. And for Leanne to tell me she recognized I'd been in an awkward position and *agree* to keep me on his project...

The problem was that I was still in an awkward position. I was in an even *more* awkward position because now I was going to have to see Rick again.

Twelve

I'D ACCEPTED THAT PIERRE, Armand, and Breton were my friends. It was strange, still, to think of them as my friend group and know that they cared about what was happening in my life. Normally, we got together for drinks once a week or so, on top of my standing plans with Mario. For reasons that now felt stupid, I'd apparently been so optimistic about my meeting with Rick that I'd agreed to have drinks with them again so I could give an update.

When I tried to cancel those plans, they resolutely refused. Frustrated, I called Mario.

"I don't want to talk about what happened with them. Can you get them off my back?"

"Nope," he said.

"Asshole."

"They want to see you. That's a good thing."

"Pierre said it was nice to see me happy," I argued. "They're not going to want to see me like this."

He sighed. "Sean, they're asking because they're concerned. They don't care that you don't have *good* news for them. They want to know you're okay and want to try cheering you up."

"Why would they—"

"Because that's what friends do," he said firmly. "If you don't want to go for drinks, it's up to you to convince them of that, but they're not going to let this go."

I groaned. "Why can't they just let me suffer in peace?"

"They care about you, whether or not you acknowledge it." Mario's tone was stern. "Look, if you want my opinion, go. Situations like this are *why* you need a support circle. You don't have to tell them what happened. You can just, like, be around people and let them show you they care."

Disgruntled, I begrudgingly showed up ten minutes late. My usual spot beside Mario was waiting for me, but as I went to sit down, Pierre stood up and moved around the table.

"Hey," he said, and threw his arms around me.

For a moment, I was so stunned, I couldn't remember what I was supposed to do with my arms. Then, slowly, I hugged him back, and something inside me cracked.

It wasn't the usual prattling chatter that night. The mood around the table was almost somber as I sat and haltingly told them about the shitshow that had been my week. I couldn't tell them everything, of course; admitting to the anger and the way I'd lost control and how afraid I'd been would require a far deeper dive into my past than I was willing to give, but it didn't matter. Mario was right, of course.

"At least there are some silver linings," Breton said when I told him what Leanne had done for me. "Like, it for sure sucks, but like... you impressed your *boss* even after everything that happened. That's amazing, Sean."

"I guess," I said, sipping my wine. "I still have to see him again, though."

"He's gonna feel worse than you do," Armand said knowingly. "Trust me."

"I overreacted," I said. "Like, I... I yelled. At him."

"You were *well* within your right to," Pierre said. "Like yeah, okay, he didn't realize how *big* a deal it was, but he knew it wasn't right. Otherwise he wouldn't've hid it from his boss."

I chewed on one of my nails, but nodded. "Yeah, that's... yeah."

Breton was watching me quietly. "You still like him, eh?"

My face burned and I clenched my jaw, but Mario touched my knee.

"It's okay if you do," he said. "You can be upset with what happened and also still think he's hot."

Armand slung an arm around my shoulders. "'Course you can. I mean, this is the guy with fuck-me cheekbones, right? The relative attractiveness of a guy correlates directly to the amount of transgressions people are willing to forgive."

I wasn't the only one who gaped at him. He sipped his drink, oblivious to the four sets of eyes on him until he looked up.

"What?" he said. "It's just science. Or... I dunno, calculus or something."

When I burst out laughing, Mario grinned and tapped my knee.

"Told you so," he murmured when I stopped giggling.

"Asshole," I muttered back, but I was smiling.

As Breton said, at least there were silver linings. Having drinks with my friends—which still felt so weird to say, *friends* instead of *friend*—helped distract me for a time. I left that night feeling less on edge than I had been.

Silver linings are still a part of the clouds, though, and the cloud that went along with it was new. After a night of drinks and laughter and hugs, I walked alone to the small studio apartment I called home. It was the same place as always—nothing had changed since I'd moved in during university—but it felt different that night. I flicked the lights on to reveal a familiar scene, but the once warm lighting felt cold as I looked at my home. It wasn't the type of place people would expect me to live, given what I did for work, but it was what I had.

It was quiet. It was empty. It was the complete opposite of the place I'd just come from, and for the first time, I didn't like that. For the first time, I didn't want to be alone. I was, though, and that meant I had all weekend to dread my meeting with Rick on Monday, imagining one scenario after another until I was twisted in daydreams and anxiety.

Unlike the previous weekend, they weren't the good kind of daydreams. I didn't have to muse on what his mouth tasted like anymore, but even though I knew how it felt to have his large hands close around my arms and what kind of electric thrill ran through me when his lips were against mine, I couldn't think of him that way.

Whatever had been between us was gone, I was sure of it. I couldn't imagine a world where Rick saw the snivelling, screaming, sinful little imp that was me and had any sort of feeling but disgust. And I'd pushed him; I'd shoved my way past him and puffed up my chest like I thought I was some sort of stereotypical tough guy. Instead of being mature and simply telling him to fuck off, I acted like I was back in the schoolyard trying to bite and claw my way home without getting kicked in the nuts.

No one would want me after that, and I couldn't blame them.

When Monday rolled around and I dragged myself out out from beneath the covers, I was exhausted. My hands shook as I got ready for work, determinedly avoiding looking in the mirror as I dressed. I didn't want to know what kind of wreck Rick would see when he got there.

Ten minutes before I was supposed to meet with him, I walked into the office. Monique greeted me warmly, as she had been every day since my one-on-one with Leanne, likely hoping I'd fill her in on what happened. I had no intention of doing that, so returned her greeting with a nod and half-smile before heading to my desk to drop off my work bag. I grabbed my notebook and drawings, refilled my coffee in the break room, and took a steadying breath before starting towards the meeting room.

I was halfway down the hallway when someone called after me. "Sean!"

"Morning, Vincent," I said, trying not to cringe.

He half-jogged up to me, holding a stack of papers. "Great timing. Leanne said you're shadowing senior staff this week, so you can file this paperwork for me. I need this done before lunch, since—"

"Not happening," I said shortly. "I have a meeting right now and a seminar to attend after this."

He raised his eyebrows. "Is that so? Because Leanne said that you're shadowing so you can learn a bit more about the process, which means—"

"I already know how to do your filing. I've done it before. Multiple times. Every time you have an excuse to pass it off on me."

Vincent's bright tone faded. "Look, if you want me to tell Leanne you weren't willing to be cooperative—"

"If you want to tell Leanne that you're the reason my meeting with Sean on behalf of Theo Barker is about to be delayed, *please* let me be there," said a voice from behind me.

My shoulders tensed as I closed my eyes for a brief moment, wishing I was still at home, asleep.

"Mr. McDougall!" Vincent said cheerfully.

"Just Rick, please," Rick said as he stopped beside me. "Anyway, I would *love* to see her reaction when you tell her you're pulling Sean out of our *very* important meeting. She is *such* a spitfire. Would you like to go now or...?"

Vincent laughed uneasily. "Seems to have been a misunderstanding. We'll catch up after lunch, Sean. Have a good meeting."

"Ugh," Rick said as he walked away. "He's a ray of sunshine, isn't he?"

My voice didn't seem to be working, so I just nodded before walking into the meeting room. After a moment, Rick followed, and the door closed with a quiet snap.

"Double fisting today?"

"What?" I asked, frowning as I looked up at him.

He had one eyebrow raised and half a smile on his lips as he put two coffees down on the table.

"Thought you could use a latte." He motioned towards one of the cups.

I stared at it, a million things rushing through my mind: confusion danced with embarrassment, which threaded itself around regret as it was swept away by anger.

How dare he?

He had lied to me. He had almost cost me my job, which would have cost me *everything*. He'd kissed me, he'd followed me, he'd made sure my boss didn't fire me for reasons I couldn't understand. He'd had *his* boss—his best friend—threaten to pull an insanely expensive project to make sure I didn't lose things he had no idea about.

And then he brought me a latte.

Me.

After I'd screamed at him, hurled horrible words at him, pushed him not once and not twice but three times. After I'd acted like a child, after I'd thrown myself in his face, after I'd all but screamed at him to fight me in the middle of a street. After he'd seen me cry, after he'd watched me lose control, after I'd stormed off.

After all of it, he brought me a latte, and I couldn't handle it.

The lattes started as an apology. I mean, he'd said it was bribery, but he'd also said Theo and Aspen decided they wanted a pool. He'd brought me a coffee every week after that, but this... this wasn't just the usual coffee. This was him wanting to apologize again. This was him wanting to sweep what happened under the rug.

And I couldn't.

I couldn't.

I didn't deserve to let that happen.

And somehow, for some surreal and unfair reason, he knew exactly what was going through my mind as I stared at the cup.

"It's just a coffee, Sean," he said.

"Right," I said, but I didn't touch it as I sat at the table.

Tension hung between us like drooping vines. Rick moved to his usual spot and sat down, then cleared his throat.

"About last week—" he started

"So, the drawings," I said, pulling them out of my book and spreading them in the center of the table.

He sighed. "Sean, please—"

"Can we not?" I asked quietly, staring at the papers in front of me.

He fell silent and those vines shifted, swaying as the air shivered with electricity. He said nothing until I felt my eyes being pulled up, first looking at his hands, then his chest, and finally into those winter sky eyes that were clouded over as they met mine.

"Sure," he said. "If that's what you want."

"I'd like to just focus on the project," I replied, looking back down at my notebook.

"Okay," he said.

"So, here are the new drawings with the changes Mr. Barker and Ms. Haws requested..."

Beside me, the latte sat untouched, and across from me, so did Rick. Gone were the flirty quips and overdramatic declarations. Gone was the laughter and the pet names and the moments where I could study the contours of his face as he studied my drawings.

It was awful.

He wasn't awful; he did exactly as I asked. I don't know why he thought I deserved such consideration, but he did, and I was grateful for it. The problem was that it made things even worse. If he'd just been a *bit* of an asshole, I could have walked away certain that I hadn't missed out on anything. Sure, he had the body of a model and a face that angels would sin for, but if he'd blamed me for what happened or insisted that we talk about it, I could have justified my anger and written him off.

But he didn't, so I couldn't, and that meant all I *could* do was feel shame.

The meeting passed in a heartbeat that lasted a lifetime. Rick asked blessedly few questions and only made one change to the drawings; he signed off on it and took a photo to send to Aspen, but said other than that, the drawings could be finalized.

"What's the next step after this?" he asked.

"Construction," I said. "I'll get everything sorted to start on the next phase of the project."

"How often do you recommend meeting?"

I bit my lip. "The first part is uneventful, to be honest. We can provide updates as often as you like, but until they pour the foundation, it's not, uh... there's not much to say."

"Right. So... you'll let me know?"

"That'd probably be best," I said, not looking at him.

"Sounds like a plan." His voice was kind and it made my heart ache. "If that's all for today...?"

"Yeah," I said.

"Great." He rapped his knuckles on the table and stood up. "Well, then. I guess I'll head out."

Out of habit, I looked up at him.

There was no anger or frustration on his face, simply a resigned sort of sadness that he tried to cover with a polite smile. Things had changed. How he thought of me had changed. I was certain that how he felt about me, whatever he had felt about me, had changed.

At least, I was until I caught that glimpse in his eyes, that little sparkle that made my breath catch in my throat and warmth rise from somewhere deep.

"Right," he said after a moment. "I'll see you when I see you, Sean."

The air in the room shifted as he walked around the table and to the door. My heart thudded painfully and my stomach flipped, but it wasn't until I heard the clear and distinct sound of the door handle turning that I managed to speak.

"Rick?" I asked quietly.

The door handle stopped turning.

"Yes?" he asked.

My spine tensed, the muscles in my back tightening so much that I was half-certain I was made of iron. My mouth was dry and I forced myself to stand up and turn towards him.

"Thank you for standing up for me last week," I said, my voice small.

He didn't say anything and I cleared my throat, though it didn't help.

"And I'm sorry," I continued, so softly I wasn't sure he heard it.

His back was to me. I couldn't see his expression, but I didn't need to. My heart was already cracked when his silence stretched on, and it splintered when he resumed twisting the handle and pulled the door open. My jaw clenched and I felt my throat tighten, anger bubbling in my stomach.

Not anger for him, of course.

Anger for me. For fucking it up. For ruining whatever chance I'd had. For the way I was and for the way I'd been made. Anger, and sadness, and the profound knowledge that this was going to be my life: anger, then pain, then loneliness.

Then, surprisingly, confusion.

Rick took a half-step out the door and stopped, twisting his neck to look from left to right. He paused, then looked left again, then swiftly stepped back into the room. The door closed with an adamant thud, he turned around, and before I could say anything else, he was in front of me.

"I'm sorry," he said intensely, staring straight into whatever soul I had left with pleading eyes.

"I am, too," I whispered, and I didn't even have time to breathe before he tilted my chin up.

Fire and pain and longing and need crushed against my lips as he kissed me. I *felt* that kiss with every bit of me, from the pit of my stomach where my anger lived to the tips of my toes to each strand of hair on my head. My body sparked, every nerve flaring at once and my skin tingling with something that was part relief, part desire, part joy and part fear, and all because of *him*.

He felt me gasp, I was sure of it. That was the only reason I could think of for him to pull back the way he did, though I didn't give myself the chance to search for answers in his eyes.

"No." Closing my fist around the front of his shirt, I tugged his face back to mine.

There was a smile on his lips that time; my eyes were closed, but I didn't need them to see that. The hand on my chin moved to the back of my neck, cradling my head and toying with my curls as his tongue slipped into my mouth. I flicked mine against it and felt the sharp intake of breath; moments later, his other hand was on my waist and his teeth grazed my lower lip.

I couldn't help it; I groaned, a low, needy sound that I was instantly embarrassed about. Shame crawled up my neck in a flush of warmth and I let go of his shirt, but before I could say anything, Rick responded. His breath caught and he made a soft noise of his own before nipping my lip again, and then his body was pressed against mine.

His chest met mine first, then his stomach, then his hips were nudging me until the back of my thighs were pressed against the table. Instinctively, I braced one arm behind me, steadying myself. My other hand shook as I reached up to touch his neck, then his jaw, then the softness of that flaming red hair.

It was like silk or satin or any number of luxurious sensations. I couldn't stop touching it, almost frustrated that his body was pressing so hard against mine that I needed to hold myself up because it meant I couldn't weave the fingers of both hands through his hair. *Almost* being the operative word. There was no way I could deny how much I enjoyed having his body pressed against mine, especially not when *my* body began to react.

And it did. I tried with everything in me to fight the contradiction of wanting his mouth and hands all over me at the same time I didn't want to end up with a fucking erection first thing in the morning in the meeting room at work.

That fight got even harder when I felt his reaction.

It also made my decision easier. I felt that telltale bulge begin pressing against me and I almost couldn't stop myself from pushing my hips forward, from grinding my body against his until I simply *had* to reach down and unbutton his jeans. I wanted it so badly; I wanted to feel the heat of his cock against my palm and I wanted to hear the noises he made when I stroked him and I wanted to see his face when I made him explode with bliss.

More than anything, though, I wanted to avoid having someone walk into the fucking meeting room and discover me with my cock hard and my mouth being ravished by a client.

"Rick," I gasped against his mouth. "We have to... I can't."

He pulled back, breathing just a touch harder than he had been, and let go of me.

"Right," he said. "Shit. Right. We're at... You... yes. No. I... *fuck*."

I pressed my lips together, trying in vain not to laugh, and failing miserably when he grinned and reached up to brush a curl off my forehead. Once he had, he leaned forward and kissed me, though it was far more chaste that time.

"We can't," I murmured. "You're a client and the project—"

"I know." He pecked my lips again before taking a step back and drawing a deep breath. "It sucks."

I brushed the back of my hand against my lips. "Yeah. But I... I need this job."

"I know," he said, even though he didn't *really* know. That was okay; it was enough that he understood, even if it meant that my body was screaming at me to let him continue where we'd left off.

"Sorry," I said, as much to myself as it was to him.

He smiled and cleared his throat. "I should get going."

Before I could nod, before I could protest, before I could tell him all the millions of things rushing through my mind, he turned and my heart jumped into my throat. Before I could think, I was speaking.

"There's no rule against being friends with clients."

He paused, then looked back at me, an eyebrow raised in amusement. "No?"

I swallowed hard and shook my head. "You said you don't know anyone here. Come out for drinks with me and my friends. We have plans on, uh, Friday. Seven o'clock. At the Grand Monk Bar. It'll be a good time."

Rick's face lit up in a way that did absolutely *nothing* to help redistribute my blood to appropriate places.

"It's a date," he said, then grinned. "But not really."

Thirteen

MARIO HAS CREATED THE group chat
    Mario has added you to the group chat
    You have left the group chat
    Mario has added you to the group chat
    Pierre: *wtf is going on*
    You: *Nothing. Bye.*
    You have left the group chat
    Mario has added you to the group chat
    Mario: *Sean has something to ask you all and if he leaves again I'm going over to his place personally and making him record it on VIDEO*
    Breton: *LOL Sean, what's up?*
    Pierre: *dont leave again my phone keeps going off when you do*
    Pierre: *hellllllllllllooooooo???*
    Mario: *Just ASK them, Sean*
    Breton: *Don't be shy!! Tell us!!*
    You: *It was just a stupid idea I had. It's stupid. Don't worry about it.*
    Pierre: *TELL US*
    Breton: *Wait wait wait*
    Breton: *Weren't you meeting with sexy redhead today?*
    Breton: *Omg is it about sexy redhead?*
    Pierre: *SEAN! the man asked a question!*
    Mario: *It's totally about sexy redhead*
    You: *Asshole*
    Breton: *I KNEW IT. What happened??????????*
    You: *Ugh. Okay. I might have done something I need help with*
    Pierre: *detaillllllllsssssss*

Breton: *He's typing moron give him a second*
Pierre: *i cant see the bubbles im on my work phone*
Pierre: *tell me if he stops typing so i can annoy the shit out of him*
Mario: *You already annoy the shit out of all of us*
Pierre sent an image
Breton: *LOL*
Mario: *no fuck u*
You: *Rick came in for his meeting this morning. That's sexy redhead's name. So he showed up and he brought me a coffee and like, wanted to keep things like they were I think? But I asked if we could just work on the project and it was just super friggin awkward the whole time. And then at the end things kind of happened. I apologized and so did he and there was some stuff and long story short I panicked and I told him there's a policy against seeing clients like that but not against clients being friends and invited him to have drinks with my friends on Friday at 7 at the Monk*
You: *So does anyone want to go out for drinks on Friday at 7 at the Monk?*
Breton: *FUCK YES I DO*
Pierre: *HOLY SHIT SEAN YOU FUCKING DID IT*
Pierre *sent an image*
Pierre: *round of applauseeeeeee i'm so happy for you*
Mario: *I'll be there :-)*
You: *You fucking better be after all this*
Mario: *LOL. It's called being an adult, Sean. Adults don't need their friends to make plans on their behalf*
You sent a picture
Pierre: *haaaaaa*
Breton: *omg Sean lol*
Breton: *this is why we love you*
Armand: *WAIT ONE FUCKING SECOND UP IN HERE*
Pierre: *lmao hey armand how was your training session*
Armand: *"Things kind of happened" Sean? WHAT KIND OF THINGS*
You: *Just things*
Pierre: *wait THINGS like THINGS-THINGS or just things*
You: *I don't even know what that means*

Breton: *You two are stupid. He was meeting a CLIENT at WORK. It's clearly just things.*

Breton: *Unless*

Breton: *Omg Sean you dirty boy what kind of things did you do AT WORK today?!*

Pierre: *is he typing? i cant see the bubbles*

You have left the group chat

Breton has added you to the group chat

Error: Mario has attempted to add someone who is already in the group chat

Error: Armand has attempted to add someone who is already in the group chat

Pierre: *not a chance in HELL are you getting away from this that easily seanie bear*

Breton: *DETAILS*

You: *I'm busy I have to go*

Mario: *That's fine. We're all still on for drinks tomorrow night anyway so you can look us all in the eye as you tell us every last dirty detail of what happened after your meeting with Sexy Rick today*

Armand: *lol sexy rick*

Breton: *mmmm can't wait to hear all about Sexy Rick*

You: *I hate all of you*

Mario: *No you don't*

Pierre: *jesus says love thy neighbour sean you can't hate us*

Armand: *Come on sean I have 45 mins before my next session and I'm bored*

I glared at my phone, though for whose benefit, I didn't know. Maybe to keep myself from laughing, since part of me did kind of want to tell them what happened. Maybe because I knew I was about to relive the moment Rick's lips had met mine, and that was going to get me thinking about him again, and I'd worked very hard during the client satisfaction seminar to *stop* thinking about him. Thank God it was a webinar and I could just sit at my desk while things, uh... calmed down.

Then again, that had been hours ago. It wasn't like I was at work anymore. It wasn't like I couldn't give the guys a quick summary of what happened and then take a shower while I thought about how Rick had leaned into me, about how I'd trembled as his breath caressed my skin, about the woodsy scent of his cologne and the heat of his tongue and...

I cleared my throat and adjusted myself before sighing and leaning against the back of my futon.

You: *You're all getting worked up over nothing but fine.*
Pierre: *YESSSSSSSSS*
Armand: *WOOOO*
Breton: *omgomgomg*
You: *So after the meeting, he went to leave and I stopped him...*

Fourteen

When bad things happened to me, I didn't question them.

Part of it was because I was certain I'd already lived the worst day of my life. In a single day, I'd lost my entire family, been told a dead son was preferable to a gay one, and had the one ray of light in my life turn his back on me when I needed him most. No matter how bad things got, I couldn't imagine something feeling worse than losing everything at once.

Most of me knew it was because I deserved it.

I didn't *want* bad things to happen to me, and I didn't necessarily handle bad things especially well, but that didn't mean I questioned them. Regardless of how I'd been made, I didn't think of myself as inherently evil. A sinner, yes, but I wasn't a bad *person*. I was just a broken person, someone who had been stitched together with mismatched parts to create a being who wasn't quite right, who wasn't quite whole, whose miserable existence was an all-around error. If anything, I questioned when *good* things happened to me, since that meant something was about to go horribly wrong.

As that week passed, I questioned a lot. I waited a lot. I spent a lot of time trying to guess what was about to go wrong, and when, and if God would allow me to hold onto any of the good things that had happened. I knew I didn't deserve them, but I thought maybe He'd go easy on me for once.

That would be a miracle, but for the first time in a long, long time, I allowed myself to hope. It was cautious, and it was fragile, and it was encased in cynicism and the expectation of devastation, but it was there.

And slowly, throughout the week, it grew.

After my meeting with Rick, I'd attended the first client satisfaction seminar. I couldn't say I'd been looking forward to them; in my mind, it was going to be a lot of lecturing about how the best customer service was provided by people who didn't have any sort of backbone with exercises on how not to look like you were dying inside when agreeing that the customer was always right. The only reason I wasn't dreading it completely was because it was a webinar, which meant I could sit at my desk with my headphones on and ignore everything around me.

Considering the state Rick had left me in, being forced to sit at my desk while things... *calmed down* was somewhat of a relief.

On top of that, the seminar wasn't that bad. It wasn't about smiling and nodding or agreeing to everything a client said, or how to suck up to clients or get them to spend more money. Instead, it focused on teaching the psychology behind the client's experience, pointing out the little things that most people didn't think of when providing a service, and how to leverage those things to create a better experience.

It was interesting enough that I was not only distracted from my thoughts of Rick, but I ended up missing most of lunch because I was making notes for the report Leanne had said she wanted at the end of the seminar. That turned into brainstorming ideas for myself and before I knew it, I was scarfing down the sandwich I'd packed for myself and rushing to meet Leanne for the first client meeting I was doing with her.

"Good timing," she said as I walked into her office. She thrust a notebook into my hands, then motioned for me to follow her to the meeting room. "Review this. I want you to take notes with the same structure Monique set up. Highlight any action items and put them on one page, then give them to Monique so she can add them to my tracker."

"Sure," I said.

"I will introduce you to the client at the start of the meeting," she continued. "You will say hello, then you will be quiet for the rest of the meeting and focus solely on listening, observing, and taking notes."

I nodded as I skimmed over the notebook she had handed me. She spoke matter-of-factly, but her tone wasn't unnecessarily harsh or unreasonable. I was there to learn from her, not to be involved in her project, and that was fine. Other people might have found her bluntness off-putting, but I appreciated the clarity.

I spent the meeting diligently following her directions, though I couldn't help myself from jotting down a few ideas as she spoke with the client for my own reference. None of them were overly serious or revolutionary, just little comments about things I would do differently if I were the lead. Once we were done, I highlighted the action items as Leanne requested and brought them to Monique.

"Do you want me to just leave this with you?" I asked as I handed her the notebook.

"If you don't mind," she replied. "I'll send you a copy of everything I type up, then give it back tomorrow."

Which she did. The only thing was, she didn't just type up the page of action items like I thought she would; when I got the email, she'd summarized the entire notes page, including the comments I'd left for myself.

I was certain that would be where the good things ended, especially once Leanne called me to her office at the end of the day on Tuesday.

"Can you explain these comments to me?" She motioned at the report as I sat across from her.

"I apologize," I said, hoping my voice wouldn't waver. "I didn't mean to overstep. It was only meant to be for my reference, and I didn't realize Monique typed up everything. I won't do it again."

Leanne raised her eyebrows. "That would be unfortunate."

A beat of wary confusion passed before I found my voice again. "Would it?"

She smiled.

I couldn't fucking believe it, but Leanne *smiled*.

"I was hoping you would explain your thought process," she said. "I was certainly not expecting to see your running commentary on the report, but these are excellent suggestions and creative solutions. So, I'd like you to explain how you came to these conclusions so we can determine if they would be feasible for the project."

I ended up staying late that night, but not a single bit of me minded. One by one, I reviewed my notes and ideas with Leanne. Not all of my suggestions worked, of course, but she jotted down at least three of them to present to the client at their next meeting.

Even so, I considered that to be a fluke, a one-off bit of luck that wouldn't be repeated. It wasn't until Thursday, when Leanne was discussing the benefits of different solar panel styles with a client, that I realized it wasn't just luck.

"What do you think, Sean?" she asked.

I looked up from my notes, trying not to look as stricken as I felt. "Me?"

She looked unimpressed. "Yes, you. What do you think the best option is?"

I cleared my throat. "Well, neither, to be honest. If you're spending this kind of money on green energy anyway, I think you should do a solar roof. It's more expensive, but the return is better and it'll address your concerns about the aesthetics."

The client leaned back in his chair, looking at me thoughtfully.

"Tell me more," he said simply, and after a quick glance at Leanne, I did.

When the meeting was done, she stopped me in the hallway before I went back to my desk.

"Please send me the information on those tiles. I hadn't heard of those before."

"Will do," I replied.

She nodded brusquely. "Thank you. And Sean?"

"Yes?"

"Keep this up. Good job."

I walked back to my desk with a lump in my throat and clouds beneath my feet. It took me a while to recognize the strange warmth floating through my chest as pride in myself.

The entire week went well, and it terrified me. The group chat Mario had created was lively and hilarious; at least three times a day, I tried not to laugh out loud at some ridiculous quip Breton made or a gif that Pierre had sent. The senior staff members I was shadowing were kind and helpful. Even Vincent took the time to sit down with me and talk me through his process instead of just handing me a stack of filing to do.

When Friday night rolled around and nothing had gone wrong, I was certain that meant Rick wasn't going to show up. Too many good things had happened; there was no way that, on top of all the successes of the week, that was going to work out for me as well. I was so convinced of that fact that I'd almost not bothered stressing about how my hair looked or what to wear before heading to the Grand Monk.

Almost.

I got there just before seven. The others were already at our usual table, two conspicuously empty chairs between Mario and Armand. Just after I sat down, the waiter strolled over. I asked for my usual glass of wine, and while the others placed their orders, I surreptitiously glanced at my phone and then towards the door.

Of course, Pierre caught me.

"It's not even five after yet," he said as soon as the waiter walked away. "Give him some time to be fashionably late."

"I was just looking around," I mumbled, but it didn't fool anyone.

"It's kind of cute," Breton said, grinning at me. "You're all nervous."

"I am not," I huffed. "It's just drinks with friends. He might not even come."

"What?" Armand said, his eyes wide. "Did he—"

"No," I said. "I just mean, it's nothing serious. It's not a date."

"Yes it is," Breton and Pierre muttered at the same time.

"It is not." I folded my arms. "One, I can't date clients. Two, if I *could*, I wouldn't invite all of you on a date with him. And three, I just have a feeling he's not going to show up, so let's just get drunk and have a good time."

"You're being ridiculous," Mario said. "Of *course* he's going to be here."

"He damn well better be," Pierre said. "I want to see what kind of guy it took to finally get our poor, dear Sean out of his shell and—"

"And now I'm having second thoughts about all of this," I muttered.

"—make sure he deserves you, Mr. Sassy Pants," he finished, then folded his arms across his chest. "If he can't put up with a bit of grilling from your friends, he's not good enough for you."

"It's like the old saying goes," Armand said sagely. "If he can't handle Pierre at his worst, he doesn't deserve Sean at his best."

"That seems incredibly unfair to Sexy Rick," Breton said. "Pierre can't even handle Pierre at his worst."

Pierre gasped theatrically. "You bitch!"

"I'm not wrong."

"Well, no, but you don't have to say it!"

Laughter rippled out from our table, mine among the loudest. I couldn't help it; the indignant look on Pierre's face was priceless.

"Just my luck," said a voice from behind me. "If it weren't for that damn train blocking traffic, I wouldn't've missed the joke."

Heat pulsed through me as I turned, though not a heat I was used to. It wasn't anger or shame or embarrassment; it was fire and happiness and excitement as I looked up, and up, and *up* to see Rick grinning down at me.

Oh, and did he look good.

His hair was styled as perfectly as it always was, and in the somewhat dim light of the bar, his eyes seemed darker and deeper than usual. He wore a blue plaid shirt, but the sleeves were rolled to his elbows and the top buttons were undone, so the white collar of the t-shirt beneath peeked out. There were models in magazines less enticing than him; and yet, for some reason, he was smiling at *me*.

"You made it," I said, unabashedly delighted.

"I made it," he repeated, pulling out the chair next to me and folding his tall body into it before glancing around the table. "Sorry I'm late. I got caught at a train crossing and then the cab couldn't find the place. I ended up getting him to drop me off a block away and just walked."

"Don't you even worry about it," Pierre said, his voice suddenly husky. "You are *right* on time."

I tried not to clench my jaw. "Uh, everyone, this is Rick. Rick, these are my friends Mario, Pierre, Breton, and Armand."

Rick smiled and I swore Breton melted slightly. "Nice to meet you all."

"And you," Armand said pleasantly. "We've heard so much about you."

Rick glanced at me. "Have you?"

"Of course," Mario said smoothly. "Sean's super proud of the project he's working on."

"Oh, that's right!" Breton exclaimed. "Rick, who the fuck do you work for?"

Rick burst out laughing. "What?"

I sighed. "I can't tell them who my clients are."

He grinned wickedly as he glanced around the table again. "Oh, so I can keep you all guessing, if I want?"

"Not if you want to impress us," Pierre said.

"I mean, I'm a little impressed already," Breton said.

"Down boy," Armand said. "Don't spook the new guy."

"You don't *have* to tell us," Mario said. "These three have just been trying to wring it out of Sean and he won't say a word, so they're convinced you work for either someone super famous or the CIA."

"I'm taking my money off the CIA," said Pierre. "No way you're a spy. They'd see you coming a mile away."

"I'm still not even convinced it's someone we've heard of," Mario said.

I tried not to laugh. I didn't keep secrets from Mario; he knew damn well who Rick's boss was.

"Maybe, maybe not," Rick said. "Tell you what. You can ask me anything and if you guess it, I'll tell you."

If there was one way to break the ice, it was with a game like that. Pierre, Breton, and Armand began firing questions at Rick so fast I could hardly keep up.

"Man, woman, or nonbinary?" Pierre asked.

"Man," Rick said.

"Is he famous?" Breton asked.

Rick smirked. "Very."

"Athlete?" Armand said, and Rick shook his head.

"Actor," Pierre said, earning another shake of the head.

"Musician?" Breton guessed, and Rick nodded with a smile.

Armand thought for a moment. "What kind of music?"

"Take a guess," Rick said.

The three of them groaned.

"Okay, is it *good* music?"

"It's decent," Rick said, laughing.

"Is he Canadian?" Pierre asked.

"Yep."

"Is he hot?" Armand asked.

"Arguably, yes."

"Gay?"

"Nope."

"Married?"

"Not... yet."

Breton slapped the table. "No fucking way!"

Pierre and Armand whirled towards him as Rick grinned.

"Who is it?" Pierre asked.

Breton's eyes were shining and he practically vibrated with excitement. "Is it Theo Barker?"

Rick nodded and Breton squealed. "I *love* him!"

"How'd you figure that out?" Armand asked.

"Oh my God, he just got engaged like... I dunno, a while ago," Breton said. "And he did this interview on CBC and he said—is it true, Rick? She proposed to him?"

"Yep," Rick said. "I helped her with it."

Before the three of them could pepper him with questions, the waiter returned with our drinks. Rick glanced at my glass. "What are you drinking?"

"Just the house red," I said.

"Is it good?"

"It's... wine."

He tried not to laugh. "Do you like cabernet?"

"Well, yeah, but—"

"Let's share a bottle." He grinned. "My treat."

I felt that unusual but incredible heat wash over me again and I smiled. "That sounds great."

And it was. *He* was. His presence at the table was natural and easy and familiar, settling in as though that chair had always been empty and waiting for him to join us. There were no awkward lulls or uncomfortable questions; his laughter entwined with ours when Breton couldn't stop himself from gushing over Theo or when Pierre gave me hell for not telling them I was working for *the* Theo Barker.

He kept my wine glass filled without asking, as though he knew I wouldn't be able to just help myself to more. Each time it was nearly empty, he reached for the bottle and poured more in each of our glasses without so much as pausing the conversation. I listened more than I talked, but I didn't mind; it meant I could watch Rick, indulging in the sight of him even if I couldn't indulge in anything more than that.

"So how do you all know Sean?" he asked at one point.

"Through Mario," Pierre said.

"Yep," Breton said. "We met… here, I think. Having drinks one night."

Armand nodded. "Mario and I met at the gym, and Sean and I met after I started hanging out with Mario."

My mouth felt dry as Rick looked past me and at Mario, amused.

"And you?" he asked.

Mario smiled. "Sean and I know each other from Winnipeg."

"Ew, Winnipeg?" Rick said, then grimaced. "I mean—"

I burst out laughing. "No, you're right. We live in Montreal now, don't we?"

"Wait, so you two moved here together?" Breton asked, frowning. "I didn't know that."

"Sort of," Mario said casually. "We both got into school here so it made sense."

"Still," Armand said. "I didn't know you guys were *that* close before living here. Like, to move to a new city together?"

"It wasn't like that." My voice came out flat and scratchy as I tried to keep the panicked worry out of it.

"I don't know about that," Pierre said loudly. "I mean, the two of you—"

"—have only ever been friends," Mario finished firmly. "You know that. Everyone at this table knows that."

"I guess," Breton said. "But also, I had no idea you moved here together."

My heart was racing and I could feel my cheeks turning red. On my right, Rick was silently watching the conversation play out, and I could only imagine what he was thinking. On my left, Mario was tense, and it was my fault. He knew it bothered me when people implied those things about us, just like I knew it bothered him. He sensed it was bothering me even more because Rick was there. And there was nothing I could do.

"It's not that weird," Mario said.

"You wouldn't be saying that if it wasn't a little weird," Pierre replied, looking at his nails. "Look, you know *we're* not going to think it's weird if you used to hook up or whatever."

"We didn't," I said, my voice shaking.

Pierre rolled his eyes. "It's not that big a deal, Seanie-bear. I mean, it explains why the two of you are such close friends. You don't have to pretend around us."

The rushing sound had started in my ears and I stared hard at my glass, trying with everything in me not to react. I was fighting so hard that when a hand touched my right knee to ground me, it took me longer than I wanted to admit to remember Mario was sitting on my left.

"Guys can also just be friends, you know." There was no laughter in Rick's voice. "Not everything has to be about who fucked or wants to fuck who."

Pierre snorted. "Okay, but you literally *just* met them. You don't know how they are."

"And yet I'm observant enough to realize this conversation is upsetting both of them and you're still pushing buttons for some reason." His hand squeezed my knee. "It also *literally* doesn't matter."

"Figuratively," Armand said.

"What?" Breton asked.

"Figuratively, it doesn't matter." Armand sipped his drink. "'Literally' doesn't make sense. I told you that, Breton. It's like when you say 'I literally died,' you didn't literally die."

Pierre rolled his eyes. "Well, you are literally the world's biggest dork."

Armand grinned. "Actually, I'm—"

"Oh, for fuck's sake," Breton groaned. "Pierre, don't get him started."

Mario laughed. "No, please do. Armand, can you literally explain it to us?"

It wasn't that funny, but everyone at the table laughed like it was Saturday night in New York. I took a shaky breath and let it out.

"Are you okay?" Rick asked.

I nodded.

"Sorry. I didn't know it was a touchy subject."

"It's okay," I said, surprised when I realized it actually *was* okay, and turned so I could look at him. "I... I'll tell you about it sometime. But it's not... we are just friends."

I was very aware of the fact that his hand was still on my knee when his lip curled between his teeth and those blue eyes seemed to sparkle in the dim light of the bar.

"Good," he said simply.

And just like that, it was. Things were still good. Rick was beside me, and he still... well. He was touching my leg, and he was smiling at me, and I was fairly certain that meant he still liked me. And yeah, I couldn't do anything about it, not without risking all the good things that were happening at work, but it was still... good.

Maybe it was time for things to turn around. Maybe I was allowed to have friends and success at work and the promise of Rick. Maybe it was time for me to feel safe and comfortable and happy. Maybe it was time for the hurt to stop, the pain to be over, the loneliness and the fear and anxiety and anger to fade.

Maybe I'd been punished enough.

For half a heartbeat, I believed it. For all of a breath, hope took over, just long enough to remind me why I should never, ever let my guard down.

"Sean?" said a soft voice.

I blinked.

Rick's lips hadn't moved. My friends were all still laughing about "literally." And no one at the table had a voice like that. No one there could make me feel like I was alone on a frigid winter day with blue lips and tears frozen to my eyelashes. No one could crush me the way the owner of that voice could. No one could punish me more.

No one else could have proved that I truly was molded from sin. That I wasn't allowed to be happy. That all the things surrounding me were an illusion set to simply remind me not to get comfortable because it could all be taken away—all *would* be taken away—at any moment.

Why else would he be there?

"Sean Stephens?"

Rick frowned. "I thought your last name was Lemieux?"

My jaw twitched and I turned away from him to see a beautiful man with pale skin and golden hair and soft lips.

"Sean," he said again.

I finally found my voice. "Don't."

Jude's lip trembled. "I thought you were dead."

Fifteen

THE WORDS SILENCED EVERYONE at the table. I couldn't see them, but one by one, I felt my friends' eyes fall on me as I stared up at the personification of Hell on Earth.

He wasn't the boy I remembered. Jude's eyes were still hazel and bright, but they were world-weary at the same time. His hair still reminded me of sunshine on a wheat field, but it was cut shorter than it ever had been when I'd known him. The delicate structure of his face was both more prominent and less; the boyishness of his cheeks had given way to something more defined, his chin jutting out more than I'd ever seen it.

The way he looked at me, though: that I remembered. It wasn't a look he'd worn often, but it was burned into my mind, framed by the haze of breath on that frozen day as we stood on the steps of his front door. Stricken, almost, with disappointment and fear and disgust all wrapped together.

That, I remembered.

Regardless of the expression on his face or the ghost of the boy I'd known beneath his skin, he'd changed. The Jude I'd known was soft in the sweetest way. He was fierce until faced with something he had to be fierce about. He was full of promises and dreams and empty words. He was generous with his friendship but not with his actions. He wrote that he loved me, that he wanted to be with me, that he'd do anything for me. He'd turned me away when I needed him.

And now here he was.

This was it. This was my punishment for daring to hope. Right when I thought I could move on. Right when I thought there was more for me in life than anger and guilt and pain and loneliness. Right when Rick had his hand on my knee and his smile in my heart.

Here he was, and he was mad.

"Aren't you going to say anything?" he said.

"Why are you here?" I asked.

"Ouch," I heard Pierre mutter behind me. "Rude."

"Shut up," Mario hissed.

Jude almost laughed. I saw it spark behind his eyes and fade, winking out of existence as he stared at me.

"Why am I here?" he repeated. "That's all you have to say?"

"Don't," I said again. "Jude, just—"

"Five years, Sean." His voice cracked. "Five *fucking* years, I thought you were dead and that it was my fault and that your dad—"

Rick's hand fell away from my knee. I didn't know if it was because I stood up and he'd had no choice or if Jude's statement had shocked him that much. It didn't matter. My heart wasn't just pounding. It wasn't racing. It was churning, spasming, dancing erratically in my chest. I could feel fire clawing up my neck and to my cheeks, part anger and part shame and all pain.

"Don't," I growled.

"Sean, wait!" Mario said urgently.

"Why did he call you Sean Stephens?" Pierre asked loudly. "This is—"

"Pierre, shut *up*!" Rick and Breton both said.

Before anyone could let any more stupidity spill from their mouths, I grabbed Jude's arm and started towards the exit. There were far more eyes on me than the ones I left behind at the table, but I ignored them all as I marched Jude to the door. He twisted beneath my grip, but didn't say anything until we were on the sidewalk and I let go of him.

"Five fucking years, Sean," he said. "And all you can ask is what I'm *doing* here?"

"I think it's a fair question," I shot back. "Considering I haven't seen you in five fucking years."

His lip twitched. "My dad lives here now."

I raised an eyebrow. "Your dad."

"My parents split up after..."

My heart dropped as his voice trailed off.

"After what?" I couldn't help asking.

His mouth twisted. "After they found out I was gay."

I swallowed hard. "How did they...?"

"They didn't know about you, if that's what you're asking," he said coldly.

"It wasn't," I said. "I was just curious."

"Yeah, well, it's none of your business." He tried to shrug nonchalantly. "At least I have my dad still."

If he intended the words to cut me, he succeeded. "How did you find me?"

"I didn't," he said bluntly. "I wasn't looking for you."

I couldn't say I wanted him to look for me, but it was like a punch in the gut all the same. "Thanks."

He glared at me. "What the hell do you want me to say? You know I fucking waited for them to find your body? Every day I waited to hear that they found you frozen in the street or in the lake or in a ditch somewhere. Do you know how much that fucked me up? Thinking you were dead and that it was my fault?"

"It wasn't your fault," I said without thinking. "And I'm not dead."

He snorted. "Yeah, well, tell that to me five years ago. And now I find out you're in fucking Montreal living it up at the bar with a bunch of—"

"So you're pissed that I'm happy instead of dead? Thanks, Jude."

"Yeah, I am. I'm pissed you let me suffer for—"

"I let *you* suffer? You—"

"You couldn't have called? You couldn't have let me know you were okay?"

"Why would I?" I snapped. "The last thing I remember, I was begging you for a place to stay after my parents kicked me out of the fucking house and you—"

"What was I supposed to do?" he interrupted. "I was scared and you—"

"*You* were scared? My dad told me to kill myself and I was outside with nowhere to—"

"Yeah, and you wanted me to fucking leave home to come with you like it was some kind of fairytale. I was a kid, Sean! What the hell was I supposed to do?"

I don't know who was more surprised when I started laughing.

"Oh, fuck off," he spat. "Do you know how much it fucking sucked without you there? It didn't take people long to figure it out, you know. And then it was open fucking season for me. I had no one and you—why the *fuck* are you laughing?"

"You had no one?" I repeated. "You were just a kid? You thought it sucked for *you*?"

"Yeah, it did," he said. "You left me there."

I wasn't sure when the laughter turned to tears, but my eyes were stinging. "I lost *everything*. Including you. And you're pissed because you, what, got your ass kicked a few more times? You have no fucking idea what I—"

"I'm not saying it didn't suck for you!" he snapped. "But you... you left me with that fucking *cult* your father started and you didn't even bother calling to let me know—"

"You didn't give a shit!" My voice echoed off the buildings, a bouncing roar that turned heads to us and away from us. "I needed you and you turned me away. Why the fuck would you think you were entitled to know where I was? As far as I knew, you didn't care if I lived or died."

"I said I loved you!" he shouted back.

"But."

His mouth fell open, but nothing came out as he frowned in confusion.

"What?" he said.

"You said you loved me, but." I shook my head, knowing if I looked at him, I would just start screaming. "My dad told me to get out, to go to conversion therapy, or to kill myself. My mom watched me leave. My sister was sobbing in her room because she didn't... I didn't get to say goodbye to her, Jude. I had no car, nowhere to go, nothing but what I could shove in my fucking knapsack before my dad got back from church. You told me you couldn't help me and now you're pissed because I didn't call you when I was just trying to *survive*."

"I was worried," he said.

"About yourself," I shot back. "It was always about you, wasn't it?"

Splotches of red appeared on his pale skin. "I didn't—"

"*You* had no one to protect you. *You* were worried. *You* thought I was dead and you were more concerned about how that affected *you* than about the fact that I might've been dead!" I shook my head. "I should've seen that. You never gave a shit about me. You gave a shit about what I could do for you."

"Don't kid yourself," he spat. "Just because I couldn't help—"

"Wouldn't."

"I *couldn't*. My parents—"

"Would've gotten divorced a couple years sooner? You would've found out you had one parent who loved you no matter what earlier?" I shoved a hand across my cheek. "Yeah, I get it, okay? I get that. You can't just fucking give up your own life for someone else. But you're sitting there screaming at me for not calling after I lost *everything* and you wouldn't help me. You used me, Jude."

"Don't fucking say that."

"Deny it, then."

"Fuck you."

I laughed. "Not in this lifetime. My life might be shit, but it's still better without you."

Anger had always been part of my life. More than once, I wondered if I purposely sought out conflict, if that broken part of me needed to feel physical pain so the emotional pain didn't seem so bad. Nursing a black eye was easier than nursing a broken heart. Ice on a split lip soothed in a way words couldn't. And so I fought, I lashed out, I hit and kicked and shoved. I protected myself. I defended myself physically when I couldn't defend myself any other way.

I'd spent years fighting for Jude. When people teased him or bullied him or threatened him, I would throw myself into the fray, between him and the anger and the hurt and the vitriol. It didn't matter to me if I was bruised or bloodied; I needed Jude to be okay. I needed to protect him. I had needed him to need me.

I'd put his protection over mine for so long that it was second nature, so when Jude hit me, I didn't even try to block it.

He hadn't been lying when he said it had been open season for him. The Jude I knew could barely muster up enough strength to swat a mosquito, let alone punch someone in the face with any sort of reaction.

That Jude was long gone, and in his place was a man who hit me hard enough that I stumbled backward.

Strangely, I felt the gold cross around my neck bounce against my skin and had the inane realization that it had popped out of my collar again. Pain blossomed along my cheekbone and dizzy yellow stars overtook my vision. If it weren't for someone grabbing me, I might have fallen to the sidewalk, but a strong set of arms steadied me as I tried to blink the light out of my eyes.

"Oh, *hell* no," I heard someone say, and the first thing I saw when the stars faded was Jude cowering as Armand stood between the two of us.

"You do *not* hit Sean," he said. "I don't give a shit who you are."

"Are you okay?" asked a worried voice.

It took another moment for me to realize the owner of that voice was attached to the arms around me, and another still for me to blink up, and up, and *up* at Rick. His face was a stony mix of concern, blue eyes clouded and the corners of his lips pointed down.

"Fine," I said stiffly, and tugged myself out of his arms.

"Are you sure?" Mario was standing on my other side, though he wasn't looking at me, instead glaring at Jude with a darkness I didn't know was possible for him. "'Cause I think I know who he is and—"

"Don't," I pleaded quietly. "Please don't make me... don't."

He tore his eyes away from Jude, worry and concern written across his face.

"No one's going to make you do anything," he said softly, and I almost cried from relief.

"You wanna call the cops or something, Sean?" Armand asked loudly. "I mean, this guy just assaulted you. Whole street full of witnesses saw it."

Jude's pale skin went pink. "What? No, I—"

"Shut up, short stuff," Rick said. "You don't get a say."

"Oh, and you do?" Jude snapped back.

I think Rick knew it was a risk to put his arm around my shoulders after I'd pulled myself away from him, but he did it anyway, and I didn't stop him.

"Yeah," he said simply. "Problem with that?"

I imagined Jude had several problems with that, but between Armand's muscles and Rick's stature, he didn't seem willing to say anything.

"Sean?" Armand asked. "What do you want to do?"

Jude's eyes met mine and I almost shivered seeing the anger and hurt filling them. It was all too relatable, all too painful, and all too much.

"Nothing," I said. "Just leave me alone, Jude."

He wrenched himself out of Armand's grip and glared at me.

"Done," he said, and this time he walked out of my life.

Sixteen

"I KNOW YOU'RE GOING to be mad," Mario said. "But I'm not sorry."

I shook my head, still holding the damp cloth to my eye. Jude had stunned me more than anything; it didn't seem like it was going to swell or bruise, but the coolness still felt nice. "Not mad."

"I had to," he said anyway. "No one knew who he was and everyone was panicking. I know you don't want people to know your business but they're your friends and—"

"It's fine," I said, leaning against the building. "I get it."

He sighed. "Pierre felt awful. He didn't know—"

"Mario."

"And Breton—"

"Seriously."

"Rick didn't say much but—"

"Please stop."

He sighed. "We're on your side, Sean. That's all I want to say, okay?"

I swallowed hard and nodded.

"Come inside and have a drink," he said.

"I'd rather not."

"They understand, okay? This is what friends are *for*."

"I know," I said. "But I kinda want to be alone right now."

"I'll walk you home."

I shook my head. "Seriously. I'm fine."

It took a promise that I'd text him as soon as I got home and again when I went to bed and *again* when I woke up before Mario agreed to let me leave. I was grateful for his concern—truly grateful, despite the fact that he needed to be concerned in the first place—but I couldn't handle going back into the bar. Not after... well, any of it, really, but especially not after knowing Armand and Rick had heard the last bit of everything I'd said to Jude. All that meant was they knew a bit more than Pierre and Breton did, since Mario had tried to give the SparkNotes version of my tragic backstory to them before bolting out of the bar to make sure Jude and I didn't kill each other.

Those were things no one but Mario had known about me. They were wounds only he knew about, and now everyone could see the scars.

I understood why he'd told them. I wasn't lying; I *wasn't* angry, and while that in itself was strange, it was stranger still that I didn't mind. It was easier, somehow, knowing that I didn't have to explain why I was the way I was. That they already knew, and I didn't have to be there while they made up their minds on how they felt about it.

After all, Mario said they were on my side, but that would be another good thing, and I didn't know if I could handle the fallout of any more good things happening to me.

He hugged me for a moment longer than usual and a moment less than I truly needed before going back into the bar to return the cloth someone had brought out for my eye. I didn't know if he'd end up staying out with the others for much longer, but that was up to him. I was beyond done with the night and as soon as he'd walked away, I started heading home.

My mind barely had time to wander before he was behind me, calling my name.

"Sean, wait."

I had to bite back a laugh. Not because it was funny, of course, but because it was so fucking absurd that I didn't know what else to do. Unlike the last time, I slowed my pace, and he caught up before I reached the end of the block.

"One day, you're going to stop running away from me," Rick said.

"Sure," I said. "It'll be the same day that you understand that when people walk away from you, it's because they want you to leave them alone."

"Oh, don't worry your pretty head about that," he replied. "I wouldn't deny you the delight of my presence."

It was harder to bite back that laugh.

"What do you want, Rick?" I asked. "I told Mario—"

"—that you wanted to be alone and that you were fine and that you'd text him eight million times so he didn't worry *his* pretty head about it," he finished. "I know. He told me that. Repeatedly."

"So why are you here?"

"I didn't think it was good for you to be alone right now."

I rolled my eyes. "And you know what I need better than my best friend who knows everything about me does?"

"I didn't say you needed it. I'd just rather make sure you're okay for myself."

I wasn't sure what to say to that. Rick didn't seem to mind my lack of response; he walked alongside me as I looked ahead, and for another block, we walked in silence.

"How much did you hear?" I asked when we reached the next intersection and had to wait for the light to change.

"We came out around the time he was talking about your dad starting a cult," he replied.

"Oh."

"Mario breezed by that little detail. Wanna tell me more?"

"Not really."

"Okay."

The light changed and we crossed the street in silence. Once we were on the other side, I sighed. "He's crazy."

"Who?"

"My dad."

"Ah."

"It wasn't a *cult*-cult. Or at least, it didn't start that way," I said. "He was a pastor. But you put someone as fanatical as him in a small, isolated town with a big religious following and things get, uh..."

"Cult-like?" Rick finished.

I smiled wryly. "Yeah."

"And Jude?"

I bristled at his name. "What about him?"

"You don't have to tell me if you don't want to," Rick said. "Just trying to understand."

For another half-block, I didn't respond. Then, almost without thinking, I started to talk.

And I told him *everything*.

I told him about my little sister and how much I missed her. How guilty I felt for leaving Lacey there. How she was talented and sweet and deserved far better than what I'd done to her, and how I was a fucking hypocrite for saying Jude should have helped me when I had done nothing to help her. I told him about my mom and how afraid I was for her, and how angry she made me, and how I didn't know if I could ever forgive her even though she tried. God knows she tried, but sending me money for college and the occasional phone call didn't make up for the fact that she took the side of that monster.

And him.

I told him about my father, the preacher, the leader, spittle flying as he spewed hate and fear. The people who had sat around me on Sundays, listening to him, following him, unquestioning and obedient. About knowing I was gay, finding out I had to hide it, thinking I was broken. Thinking I was wrong.

He listened as I told him about Jude and how he'd come into my life. How I'd loved him.

How I'd left him.

He listened as I relived the worst day of my life, speaking with the disjointed disconnect I had to in order to get through the story without crying. I told him about walking away from Jude's house certain I was going to freeze to death and how I'd only made it to the bus station because I slipped and fell on the side of the road, and some Good Samaritan who hadn't heard about what a perverted sinner I was pulled over to give me a ride.

My apartment wasn't far enough to tell him the entire story while we walked. A lot of it, yes, but not all of it. More importantly, I was so distracted by talking with Rick that it didn't cross my mind that we were walking to my *apartment*. It wasn't until we were there and I looked at the building that I realized he might... well.

"So how did Mario come into the picture?" Rick asked, not realizing I'd stopped walking in front of a set of stairs. "I mean, he obviously knows all of this already."

"Uh... that's a long story," I said. "And this is my... my building."

He turned, a wicked smirk playing across his lips. "Don't worry. I won't think any less of you if you invite me in on the first date."

I tried to laugh, but all that came out was a cough. "It's... it's not a date."

"Because of your job," he clarified.

"Right."

"Not because you don't want it to be a date."

I cleared my throat. "Well, it would have been a pretty disastrous date if it was."

He smirked. "I dunno about that. You got me back to your place after."

I swallowed hard. "I... yeah."

He stepped forward, the playfulness fading from his face. "Am I making you uncomfortable? Because that's not my intent. If you don't want me to come in, that's—"

"I do," I said, my face flushing. "I... I can't. You can't."

"There's no expectation of anything," he said. "Not unless you want there to be."

Oh, God.

"Rick, I *can't*," I whispered. "Want has nothing to do with it. I want..."

"What do you want?"

I couldn't speak. Instead, I shook my head.

"Okay." He took my hand. "It's okay."

"I don't want you to see my apartment." My voice cracked and suddenly I was trying to wipe my face as Rick tried to figure out why I was fucking crying again.

"Sean," he whispered.

"I'm sorry," I tried to say, but the words barely squeaked past the lump in my throat.

It didn't matter what I said, though. In the best possible way, Rick didn't care. Before I could pull myself away from him, his grip on my hand tightened and he pulled me forward, strong arms wrapping around me.

He was so tall that my head fell naturally on his chest, and he held me against him so fiercely that I could feel his heart pounding through his skin. I choked back a sob, feeling my face turn red as his arms tightened even more.

"I'm a mess," I said. "I'm sorry."

"You're not a mess," he murmured. His lips brushed against the side of my head and a soft breath tickled through my hair. "You're okay. I've got you."

He had me.

"Why?" I tried to ask, but my heart had heard his words and reacted before my mind could even have a say. The wall that had been doing a piss-poor job of holding back my emotions to begin with shattered, and when he kissed the side of my head again, I just couldn't any more.

I was so tired.

The tears were a downpour, a flood that I couldn't control, and I buried my head against him. He spoke softly, though I had no idea what he said, and held me tightly. Soft hands rubbed my back and he swayed, rocking me, soothing me, treating me like I was precious and worthy and important, and I just *couldn't*. I couldn't hold it back.

In his arms, I broke, and against his chest, I rested, and for the first time in so, so long, I felt right.

I felt safe.

The way he held me almost made me want to cry forever, but I didn't. Eventually the tears ran out, and my breathing steadied, and I shivered in his arms. I swallowed back the lump in my throat, certain he was going to let go, but he didn't. He waited, holding me, touching me, his breath warm against my cheek, until I pulled away.

Even then, he reached forward and touched the side of my face. His thumb ran along my cheek as he directed me to look up at him.

"I'm sorry," I said again. "I'm... you don't... you don't deserve to put up with this."

"Put up with what?"

I half-laughed and shrugged. "This. Me. The fucking baggage."

The shadow of a smirk crossed his lips. "I'm not 'putting up' with anything. I *want* to know you, Sean."

"Why?"

"Because I like you, dummy."

I burst out laughing. "What is *wrong* with you?"

"What?" He looked affronted.

"You…" I shook my head. "Jesus, Rick. Your taste is shit."

"I have amazing taste," he shot back. "As I've proven time and time again."

"You seem to think so, but here you are," I said, and the smile faded from my face. "I've been an ass to you. I keep telling you we can't date. You just got caught up in the drama of my entire fucking life which *literally* involves a cult and being disowned by my entire family. And now…"

My voice cracked again and I glanced at the building.

"Now what?" he pressed.

Now what.

Wasn't that just it, though? *Now* what? I'd broken in his arms and cried against him. I'd shoved him and yelled at him and turned him away. I'd revealed myself to him, I'd involved him in the soap opera that was my life, I'd subconsciously done everything I could to show him he was wrong, that I wasn't worth knowing, that he deserved better than… than whatever I was.

But there he was. He was still standing there, still holding me, still touching me. And there was one thing left, one more thing that could make him walk away.

I sighed. "Come in."

"What?"

I turned on my heel and started up the steps, digging my phone out so I could text Mario and tell him I'd gotten home safe.

"Come in if you want," I said without looking at him, and if it weren't for the way my hands shook as I unlocked the door to the building, I might have almost seemed calm.

Seventeen

I WAS SEVENTEEN WHEN my world shattered.

Instead of focusing on applying for college and getting ready to graduate high school, I was focused on not freezing to death. Winter was a bad time to get kicked out of the house in general, but winter in Manitoba was downright dangerous. It took months before I got feeling back in the frostbitten tips of my fingers and toes; it was only luck that kept me from losing them completely.

After leaving Jude's house, I didn't know where to go. I walked aimlessly, colder on the inside than I was on the outside, and would have probably just stayed lying in that snow-filled ditch I stumbled into if it wasn't for Mr. Jones.

He saw me fall and pulled over to check on me; when he realized how cold I was, he ushered me into the warmth of his sedan and blasted the heater.

"It is too dang cold to walk, Mr. Stephens," he said. "Now, let me drop you off wherever you're going. Heading home, or...?"

"The bus station," I said, teeth chattering.

He raised an eyebrow. "Do your folks know you're going to the bus station?"

"Yeah," I said.

He regarded me carefully, but seemed to decide that the preacher's son couldn't possibly be lying to him and put the car in drive.

My skin ached as it was battered by the hot air, but by the time we got to the bus station, I was mostly warm. Mr. Jones parked in front of the station doors and turned to me.

"You're certain your parents know you're not home?"

"I promise, Mr. Jones."

He nodded, his lips pressed together. "Right. Stay warm then, Mr. Stephens."

I swallowed the bile that jumped into my throat when he called me that. It was a tired old cliche, wasn't it? "Call me Sean, Mr. Stephens is my father."

But having his name sickened me.

I took the bus to Winnipeg because there was nowhere else to go. There was no point in going to one of the other little towns that peppered northern Manitoba, and I didn't have all that much money. I had very little money, actually, and for a little while I wondered if I should've just taken whatever Jude offered.

Only for a little while, though. Mainly because the thought of him brought anger so strong it shook whatever soul I had left.

Getting to Winnipeg didn't solve my problems, of course. I knew no one. I had nowhere to go. Homelessness was thrust upon me completely; at seventeen, with no credit card or fake ID, I couldn't have rented a motel if I'd had the money for it. There was probably some cash-only place somewhere that wouldn't ask questions, but I barely knew my way around.

I managed to sleep at the bus station without question for a night; for all intents and purposes, I still looked like a normal kid. Of course, when the night shift showed up on the second day and realized I was still there, the jig was up.

"This ain't the youth shelter," said the security guard as he escorted me out.

"Right," I said. "And, uh... if one wanted to know where the youth shelter *is...*?"

It wasn't too far from the bus station; I barely lost feeling in my fingers by the time I made it there.

God might not have made me, and the devil might not have cared about me, but there was some level of divine providence that night. They had room, they said, and just like that, I had a place to stay. At least, I had a place to stay for a few months, until I turned eighteen and had to find one of the regular homeless shelters to stay at.

Having solved the immediate concerns of shelter, warmth, and food meant I had more time and energy to expend on getting caught in an all-encompassing downward spiral. If there's anyone in the world who knows how to get contraband in a youth shelter, it's the kind of kids who need to use a place like a youth shelter.

I mostly stayed away from the drugs; going from a middle class family to the streets meant that alcohol was enough of a temptation, and it was a hell of a lot cheaper. It got even cheaper when one of the other kids in the shelter introduced me to the guy who dealt with fake IDs so I could go with them to the bar.

"What name you want on it?" he asked.

"Sean Ste—" I stopped myself before I finished. "Or, uh..."

The guy grinned, yellow teeth framed by black gaps. "Didn't think of the name beforehand, eh? S'okay, lots of you don't. Go with the same first name. Different last name. You got a favourite rock star or something?"

I thought quickly, then cleared my throat. "Lemieux."

"Lemieux?" the guy repeated. "Like the hockey player?"

My face burned red and I nodded. He smirked and jotted it down. "Didn't peg you for a Penguins fan."

I swallowed and nodded, not willing to admit that the main reason I'd become a Pittsburgh fan was because Mario Lemieux was practically everything I wanted in a man.

Going to the bars meant I could get drunk for a lot cheaper; going to the gay bars meant I could drink for free if I played my cards right. More than once, I stumbled back to the youth shelter past curfew and had to sleep in the lobby instead of my bunk; more than once, I sat bleary-eyed and hungover in front of one of the social workers the next morning, nodding as I listened to the lecture about the dangers of alcohol and how irresponsible I was to be putting myself in the situations I was.

I'm sure they all breathed a sigh of relief when I turned eighteen and left. One less kid to lecture. One more bed to give to someone more worthy of their help.

It didn't take much time before I longed for the relative comfort of the youth shelter. The regular shelters were full to bursting and most nights,

I couldn't get in. The other people were ruthless; I was robbed twice on the first night I got a bed.

Twice. In one night.

I barely had enough to fill my backpack. At least it taught me not to get attached to anything. If I didn't have a favourite hat, it didn't matter if it got stolen. So what if my shoes went missing? So what if I didn't have a bar of soap or mittens or clean socks? So what if I lost my family and friends and any semblance of comfort?

What did it even matter?

I wasn't proud of the next part of my life. I wasn't proud of much of my life, but especially so for the next part. I didn't have much choice, but I didn't... it wasn't something I liked to talk about. Or think about. Or remember. I spent more than one night on the streets, and I spent more than one night doing things that kept me off the streets and in someone else's bed.

That was all anyone needed to know.

It was the lowest of the lows. Finally, there was a day that I wondered if my father's suggestion to off myself would just be easier. I had no one. I had nothing. I was worth even less.

Why was I bothering?

Instead of deciding, I went out drinking that night, and I puked on some guy's shoes.

He was a couple of years older than me, but that didn't concern me in the slightest. He could have been two or three times my age and it wouldn't have mattered. He was gorgeous, with naturally tan skin and big brown eyes and teeth that sparkled when he smiled.

I went home with him. I thought he... I was very drunk. I mean, I puked on his shoes. When he didn't immediately deck me or shove me away in disgust, I thought... well.

After we stumbled into his apartment, I asked if I could borrow his shower and brushed my teeth. Once I was cleaned up, I wrapped a towel around myself and walked out, sobering up just enough that I was pretty sure I could make it through whatever he wanted to do to me without puking again.

He was sitting on the couch, scrolling idly through his phone, and looked up when I exited the bathroom. For a long, painful moment, he looked at me, then sighed.

"That's what I thought," he said.

"What?"

He stood up and walked into his bedroom. I wasn't sure if I was supposed to follow or not; before I could decide, he reappeared holding a folded pair of pajama pants and a t-shirt.

"Here," he said.

I took them from him, looking up with confusion.

"Clothes," he said. "Put them on."

"What... what are you going to do?" I asked uncertainly.

"Make you get dressed and give you some blankets for the couch," he replied. "Then go to sleep."

I was certain it was some sort of weird sex game or something. Sighing, I got dressed, then returned to the living room. "What do you want me to do?"

He pointed at the stack of blankets he'd put on the couch and looked at me sternly. "Go to sleep."

"But—"

"Sleep. In here. By yourself," he said pointedly. "And my room is off limits."

When he walked away, I stared at him, so stunned I couldn't bring myself to move.

"What's wrong?" he asked without looking at me.

I opened my mouth, then closed it.

"What's your name?" I asked.

He turned and smiled. "Mario. Yours?"

I laughed. "Sean Lemieux."

He snorted. "For real?"

I swallowed and shook my head. "But it's what I go by."

He smiled kindly. "Well, we'll make it your real name one day."

Mario found me when I had nothing. I had no one. I had no hope. He took me in and cleaned me up; he gave me the chance I needed. It took a mix of patience and exasperation for him to get me to finish my high school diploma. It took tough love and a lot of tears for him to convince me to answer my mom's phone calls. It took him pushing me to get me to apply for a job and then for college. It took a lot of reasoning and long nights for him to even somewhat convince me to let go of the guilt of not going back for my sister.

More than once, I asked him why he'd done it. It took a long time before he told me about his version of Jude: the boy he'd loved as a teenager. The boy whose parents had thrown him out. The boy who decided it wasn't worth bothering with life anymore.

It would have been a beautiful fairytale romance if we'd fallen in love, but we didn't. We loved each other fiercely, but we weren't in love. I owed him too much, and he saw too much of his Jude in me. He was proof that soulmates didn't have to be lovers. He was part of my life; inextricably bound to me by his choice and by my need, and neither of us would have it any other way.

We moved to Montreal together; he wanted to be a hairdresser and I wanted nothing more than to be an architect. I always had, and it was only with his support that I even considered it a possibility. I did responsible, mature adult things like buying a futon so I didn't have to keep sleeping on the couch—it might not have been a bed, but it was what I could afford—and reminded myself that I could never, *ever* end up back in a place like the one Mario had found me in.

There would never be another Mario, and I would never get a second chance.

That thought consumed me. Everything in my life became about succeeding. I studied constantly. I worked when I wasn't studying. Every cent I could save, I did. I refused, I absolutely *refused* to end up on the streets again, fighting to get a bug-ridden cot in a shelter or pressing myself against the sleaziest-looking man in the bar that would open his bed if I opened my mouth.

I would *never* end up like that again.

Eighteen

RICK'S BACK WAS TO me. He hadn't looked at me at all while I was telling him the rest of the story.

Well, maybe he had. I couldn't bring myself to look at him, so I didn't actually know.

When I finished talking, he didn't say anything, and it was only when I glanced up that I noticed he was facing the other direction. I didn't know what he was looking at, really, but his head turned slowly as he took everything in.

Bare walls.

A futon with one blanket and two pillows.

Two kitchen chairs.

A table that didn't match.

An IKEA lamp.

A laptop sitting on top of a cardboard box in front of the futon.

One coffee maker, a toaster oven, a refrigerator, and a cooking range on the counter top. Four bowls, three plates, a handful of mismatched cutlery, two mugs, and one glass. A single cutting board, one knife, a frying pan and a pot.

Tucked away was the miscellany: toiletries and towels, clothes, a small set of carefully maintained Tupperware containers. The sundries of life, barely enough to fit into the cardboard box I used as a coffee table.

That was all I owned.

The moment stretched on. Still, Rick didn't speak, and as his silence grew, so did the rush of blood pulsing in my ears. I watched the back of him, broad shoulders almost slumped beneath his shirt, and felt my stomach start to curl with aggravation.

I *knew* there'd be an end. I *knew* eventually I'd tell him something that was too horrible, too bothersome, too much for him to handle. And I accepted that might happen. I'd accepted it the moment I told him he could come inside. Hell, I'd known it might happen weeks earlier. Months earlier. All that time we'd spent flirting and meeting and discovering each other... I knew it had to come to an end. He deserved better than the fucked up excuse for a tragic figure that was me, and he was going to realize that, and I'd told myself that was okay.

Given that the devil made me, one would think I was a better liar, but I wasn't.

Still, it was my own fault for being stupid enough to believe myself. I swallowed hard, trying to keep my throat from closing, trying to stop the crawling heat from burning up my neck. My jaw clenched as I tried to hold it in, as I started reminding myself I'd been stupid for hoping, for believing, for thinking that *anyone* would... well.

When he finally turned around, I stared at him steadily. I was going to face him while he told me he was done and that he'd changed his mind, that I wasn't worth the trouble. I could feel tension pulling at my tendons, my back as hard as stone and my hands in fists.

"Well, it's a good thing I'm here," he said.

I wasn't expecting that.

"What?" I asked, my fists unfurling.

Rick smiled. There was more sadness to it, a sobriety that was almost grim, the curl of his lips a bit more subdued than usual. But it was still a smile, and it still made my stomach flip, and it still confused the shit out of me.

"It seems like you've had it rough," he said. "And even though, as you know, I like it rough—sometimes, Sean, darling, let's be clear about that since you'll need to sweet talk me once in a while too—I don't like that you've *had* it rough. So luckily, I'm here, since I think it's about time you had something good happen to you."

The fucking arrogant...

"And you think you're that good thing?" I asked.

He grinned. "I know I'm that good thing."

I gaped at him, my mouth opening and then closing.

"That was funny, Sean," he said after a moment. "You can start laughing now."

I did, sort of. My body was confused; my heart was still pulsing and there was anger still bubbling through my veins, but my shoulders had slumped and my head felt light. I choked on what might have been a laugh but might have also just been a cough. My mind was racing, dizzy with emotions and feelings and contradictions. I shook my head, and then Rick was standing in front of me again.

"Sean," he said firmly, grabbing my hands.

"Why?" I asked. "I don't deserve—"

"Oh, don't even start with that," he huffed, and then he kissed me again.

And I kissed him back.

I couldn't help it. His mouth was an *addiction*, a sweet relief that I hadn't even realized I'd been craving. Eager lips moved against mine and I was lost, my head spinning, my body shaking off its confusion and settling on desire and need. It wasn't until Rick's arm slipped around my waist and pulled me closer that I had a gasping thought.

"Rick," I said against his lips. "My job—"

"Don't start with that either," he said, and I clung to him as his tongue slipped into my mouth.

Oh, but he was good at distraction.

"Please," I half-protested.

He stopped. Of course he stopped. The second he felt my hesitation, he moved his mouth away from mine. If I let go of him, I was sure he'd let me pull away. If I told him to leave, he would, and my heart almost burst knowing that, somehow, this man had my trust.

"I can't lose my job," I said.

"You won't," he said firmly. "I promise you, it's not—"

"You are a client. I'm... it's in the handbook. I could—"

He touched my cheek, silencing me. "One, I'm not your client. Theo is your client. Two, I'm not going to out you to your boss. Three..."

He hesitated, his face uncertain.

"What's three?" I asked.

"The number after two."

I pressed my lips together and tried not to laugh, but it was futile, and Rick grinned.

"Three is that... well." That same quiet solemnity took hold of him. "I won't pretend to know what you need or... or anything like that. I don't know what's best for you, as much as I want to. But..."

I bit my lip. "But?"

He sighed. "Look, there's more to life than just surviving."

"I know, but—"

"Your job is important, I know. And your apartment is..." He glanced away, eyes looking at the bareness of the space again. "You've had more than your share of shit thrown at you, okay? So I think you need this. I think you need it more than you need to worry about someone at your job possibly finding out. You need someone to show you how fucking important you are."

A beat passed where I was captured by the blue of his eyes as he stared intensely into mine.

"I want to be the person who shows you that, Sean. And for fuck's sake, if something happens because of it, I'm not gonna let you end up on the street. Darling, you *saw* how many bedrooms I put into Theo's house, and he doesn't even know where all of them are. I'll just sneak you into one of those. Throw a bookcase in front of the door and bam. Secret room."

There was a tear streaking down my cheek as I started laughing. He wiped it away, grinning, and before I could think about it any more, I kissed him again.

And again.

And when he slipped his tongue in my mouth again, I didn't stop him, because he was right. I needed this. I needed it more than anything.

I needed him.

I eagerly met his tongue with mine, relishing the slight coolness that tickled my cheek as Rick inhaled sharply. Once he recovered, he nipped my lower lip, tugging it with his teeth before kissing me harder.

The hand that had been cradling my cheek traced along my jaw, fingers tickling down my neck and to my shoulder. The action made me shiver, each spot he touched sending a tingle of anticipation through my skin.

I don't know how his lips and fingertips alone made me react the way I did, but my cock was already starting to stir.

And so, apparently, was Rick's.

He groaned as I moved my hand to his chest, indulging myself in the feel of soft fabric and hard muscle beneath my palm.

And, oh God, did I like how that felt.

"Are you okay?" he murmured against my mouth.

"Yes," I gasped.

I felt him smile. "Because I can slow down or stop if you—"

"Don't do that to me," I groaned, and he had to stop kissing me for a moment as he laughed.

I couldn't help smiling as he did, and that made him grin even more.

"Your smile is gorgeous," he said. "Damn, Sean."

He must have known I had a hard time taking compliments. He spared me the anxiety of having to respond by capturing my mouth again. His hand splayed against the small of my back and he flexed his fingers, a gentle hint that he wanted me closer, and closer, and closer until our hips were pressed together and I could *feel* his reaction.

The vibration of a moan rumbled against my lips. Rick trembled as I felt the distinct twitch of his cock through the layers of denim between us.

The feeling of his bulge against mine was thrilling in a way that was breathtaking and all-encompassing. The way he touched me drove me crazy; the way he tasted consumed me. Hands were moving on my back and his hips were grinding forward and I was already so intoxicated with him that I couldn't think.

Instinct and need guided me. There was no distinct thought that led me to start undressing him; one moment I was relishing the feel of his body against mine and the next, my hands were between us and working the buttons of his shirt loose. His lips never parted from mine, so I felt him smile as I popped one button after another, my fingers betraying how much I wanted him.

How much I needed him.

He untangled his arms from around me, taking half a breath to cradle my head with his hands as he kissed me hard. I knew what he was intending to do, but I still whimpered as he pulled away, not quite ready to lose the taste of his kiss. When I opened my eyes, he was smiling again, his eyes filled with desire and humour and... I didn't know what else.

Well, I did, but I couldn't allow myself to believe someone would look at me like that.

Rick grabbed the hem of my long-sleeved shirt and lifted it over my head. The cross around my neck caught the collar, tugging gently before it loosened and fell back against my skin. I shivered, realizing how very warm I was and how very cool the air felt as it caressed my back and chest.

My shirt fell forgotten to the floor, but he didn't return to my arms right away. Instead, he looked, eyes travelling down my body and taking in the sight of me. I shivered again, though it had nothing to do with the temperature that time, and those winter eyes met mine again.

"Damn, Sean," he said again, appreciation dripping from his voice.

I laughed a little, heat rising from my collarbone up my neck and to my cheeks. Nothing about me warranted that kind of reaction, in my opinion, but damn if it didn't make me feel good.

"Now you," I said.

"Now me," he agreed, shrugging the unbuttoned shirt off before unceremoniously stripping off the t-shirt beneath, letting it drop to the floor as I gaped at the perfection revealed before me.

He worked out, that much was clear, but not so excessively that he was intimidating. A few freckles dotted his skin; he probably had less of them than I did. There was a small amount of reddish-brown hair highlighting his defined pecs and his stomach was flat and firm. I was fairly certain that the best feeling in the world would be having those toned arms wrapped around me.

"Sean?" he asked when it was obvious all I could do was stare.

"Damn," I breathed, and he burst out laughing.

"Come here," he said, and that invitation was apparently what it took for me to break out of my stupor.

For someone who had joked *multiple* times about how rough he liked it, he was incredibly tender. He took me in his arms again, both of us letting out sighs that were a mix of both longing and relief as first our skin, then our lips, touched. I ran my hands down his arms and back up his stomach and chest, using my palms to read him, memorize him, worship him. As I did, he used his body to guide me towards the futon, our bodies caught in a stumbling sort of dance until we reached the mattress.

I made to get onto it, but he caught my wrist and stopped me before moving his hands to my belt. I exhaled steadily as he unbuckled it, shivering at the sound of leather swishing past the metal clasp and the soft jangle as it hung loose. My cock throbbed as he worked the button of my jeans loose, and I knew he was about to find a mess of pre-cum staining my boxers.

His eyes met mine as he unzipped my fly, a silent but dedicated check-in to make sure I was okay. I was—I was more than okay, I was soaring through clouds and experiencing what heaven must have been like—and he licked his lips before slipping his hand into my jeans.

When his hand cupped my cock, I thought I might explode.

"Fuck," I hissed.

Rick grinned. "I'd love to, darling, but first I'm gonna need these to come off."

A few easy nudges and a shift of my hips was all it took for the jeans to fall to the floor; his hand didn't even have to leave my cock. I was immensely grateful for that, especially as he traced his fingers along my length.

"Now you," I managed to gasp as he teased my cock through the fabric of my boxers.

He grinned. "Now me."

His jeans met mine on the floor and this time, instead of staring like a blank-faced moron, I checked him out unabashedly before touching him. I could feel the messy, wet spot on my boxers from my leaking cock, but I definitely wasn't the only one. A patch of wetness spread from his tip, only slightly darker than the fabric of the black boxer-briefs he wore, everything hugging him just tightly enough that I could see the perfect outline of his cock.

I explored him, mimicking the way he'd traced my cock through my boxers. My breath caught in my throat and I licked my lips as I felt his heat and thickness before teasing my fingers along his balls. He groaned as I did, but before I could go any further, he caught my wrist.

"Get on the—" He stopped, then twisted his mouth to the side playfully. "I refuse to acknowledge this thing as a bed, but it'll have to do for now."

Minutes earlier, his comment about my futon would have sent a spike of anger through me. Now, though? It was nothing. I laughed and got onto the futon, sliding back and looking up at him.

It was amazing how fragile his stature made me feel. I wasn't short or especially small, but Rick towered over me and the broadness of his chest and shoulders exuded power. As he followed me onto the mattress, I wondered again how true his claim of liking it rough was; at the same time, part of me inherently trusted that he wouldn't hurt me.

I don't know why. I hardly trusted anybody. But Rick... I couldn't help it.

He crawled forward, eyes never leaving mine, until I had no choice but to lay on my back as he hovered over me. Strong arms ended up on either side of me and he used his knee to part my legs before lowering his head so he could kiss me. His body pressed against mine again, mostly supported by his arms so he wasn't crushing me. I couldn't stop myself from straining upwards and groaning as he purposefully pushed himself against me.

God, he felt amazing.

"How are you doing?" he whispered against my mouth.

"So good," I breathed.

"What's the limit here?"

"What limit?"

He smirked and nipped my lip. "Is there anything you don't want me to do to you? Is there anything you *do* want me to do? Or that you want to do to me?"

I opened my eyes and stared up at him.

"I... uh." I coughed. "I don't know. I... what do you want?"

"You, mostly, however that happens to be."

I glared at him and he burst out laughing. "I'm trying to ask if you're a top or a bottom." He grinned wickedly and flicked his thumb across my bottom lip. "Not that we have to go there tonight. I have a whole bunch of things I'd like to do to you first."

I felt heat rising in my cheeks, partly because of what he was asking and partly because my mind was so preoccupied by literally everything else that I could barely remember how to speak, and I licked my lips again. "Right. I, uh... I like both."

The startled look of surprise on Rick's face made me blush even harder until a smile radiated from his face.

"I knew you were made for me," he murmured, then kissed me again.

"How?" I asked.

He nipped at my lip. "'Cause I like both too, darling."

He punctuated his statement by pressing his cock against mine again, harder this time. I groaned, the muscles in my stomach tightening as my cock *ached*. He knew how much I needed him, somehow; maybe from the way my cock couldn't have possibly gotten any harder, or maybe from the way I was straining up against him, or maybe from me whispering that I needed him. It was probably that last thing, though my words were so quiet I couldn't quite believe he'd heard them.

He tore his lips away from mine so he could press them against my neck, and then my collarbone, and then my chest. He licked my nipples and nuzzled against the patch of hair on my chest before moving his mouth to my stomach and nibbling his way down to my belly button. It was around that time that he moved his hands to my hips and started pulling my boxers down, moving his head away from me only when he had to shift so he could take them off completely.

He stopped when he did, taking his time as he brushed his eyes over me, looking over every inch of me before catching my eye again and grinning.

"Gorgeous," he said. "Now me?"

I grinned and nodded.

His cock was phenomenal. I mean, by that point, I almost expected it to be. Every inch of him was perfection, so why should those inches be any different? But I still marvelled at it as he revealed it to me; the way it stood proudly out from his body, the reddish-brown curls of hair at his base, the glistening of his pre-cum as he watched me drool over him.

All too soon and yet not soon enough, he was moving again. My cock twitched as he kissed the spot my waistband used to be, and again when I felt his breath against me. Moments later, the wetness of his tongue was massaging the underside of my shaft.

He licked every inch of my cock, teasing my head with his tongue before kissing his way back down to my base. I nearly lost my mind when he licked my balls before sucking on them, and when he got back to the head, there was even more pre-cum for him to clean up before he finally took me into his mouth.

It was heaven. Or, at least, as close to heaven as someone made by the devil could experience. He looked up at me, blue eyes shining as he bobbed his head and cupped my balls and used his mouth to worship every inch of me.

For a while, I couldn't bring myself to touch him, like if I felt that silky hair beneath my palms, I might wake up and discover it was all a dream. I wasn't sure how someone managed to smirk with a cock in their mouth, but Rick was apparently capable of it, and after a while he grabbed my hand and moved it to his head.

I groaned when he did; my cock twitched in his mouth and I knew I wasn't going to last much longer. I pushed his hair off his forehead and rested my hand against his head, watching him as a fiery pressure began to climb through my entire body. I tried to prolong it, to keep that pulsing feeling as long as possible so I could keep watching Rick suck my cock, but of course, it got to be too much and I had to tilt my head back.

"Oh my God," I gasped. "Oh my fucking *God*, Rick."

I learned just then that he *loved* hearing me say his name like that. His groan was muffled by the fact that my cock was halfway down his throat, but that didn't matter; I didn't need to hear it to feel that sound vibrating through me. My entire lower body started to buzz and I gasped, my eyes squeezing shut as it became more than I could take.

"Coming," I groaned.

My hands tightened involuntarily as I thrust up into his mouth, clinging to him like if I let go, I was going to fall off the end of the earth. My entire body tensed, the muscles in my stomach clenching as I thrust into Rick's mouth, filling it, spilling cum on his tongue and down his throat. I grunted, trying with everything in me to control myself and failing, happily failing, as my ears started to ring and a pleasurable ache overtook my lower body.

Rick pulled away and swallowed, wiping a hand across the back of my mouth. I kept my eyes closed, trying to catch my breath as I felt him move up on the mattress. When I opened my eyes and turned my head, he was beside me, a soft smile on his face.

"You okay?" he asked, running a tender hand through my hair.

I caught a split-second glimpse of the shock on his face as I shifted suddenly to face him. Before he could say anything, I kissed him boldly, muffling the soft but surprised noise he made. My tongue slipped into his mouth and my hand slipped down his body to find his dripping cock. He groaned as I stroked it before taking my hand and my lips away.

"Now you," I whispered, and pushed him onto his back.

Nineteen

IF IT WEREN'T FOR someone stirring beside me the next morning, I would have slept until noon.

Anger and bliss and humiliation and hope had all taken their toll on me; my emotional exhaustion was so thorough and so sudden that I'd fallen asleep only a short while after making Rick come down my throat. I barely got to revel in the fact that I'd done such a good job, he was quiet for a good ten minutes after he finished.

That was probably a good thing, since it meant when I was half-asleep on his chest and he tugged the blanket over us, I didn't have enough energy to marvel at the fact that he wanted to stay the night with me. I may not have understood *why* Rick wanted me, but I had no doubt that he truly *did* want me.

After all, it took a fair amount of dedication for a six-foot-four man to willingly sleep on a futon that his five-foot-nine lover could barely stretch out on.

I slept the night through without so much as moving. I knew that because when the cautious movement of someone trying not to wake the person sleeping beside them started, I was still curled up against Rick's chest with his arm cradling my shoulders.

When I opened my eyes, he grimaced.

"Sorry," he whispered.

"S'okay," I mumbled, trying to stifle a yawn as I pulled away from him. "You leaving?"

He raised an eyebrow. "Are you telling me to?"

I shook my head, unsuccessful in stifling the yawn, and he chuckled as he untangled his arm from around me and flexed his fingers.

"I was just enjoying having you in my arms so much that I figured I'd try to wake this one up," he teased. "You know, so I could actually *feel* you."

I smiled groggily. "Sorry."

"Don't be." He shook his hand and wiggled his fingers a few more times. "Can I ask you a question?"

"Hmm?"

He glanced at my neck. "You wear that cross."

My shoulders tensed. "And?"

"And way back when, you told me the church hates you."

I didn't say anything.

"Are you still, like, going to church and stuff?" he asked.

"No."

"So why wear it?"

I half-shrugged. "Habit, I guess."

He didn't believe me, but didn't press the issue. "What are your plans for the day?"

The question startled me almost as much as the sudden hope that he wanted to spend the day together. "Uh... nothing. You?"

"Shopping," he replied.

The hope deflated. "Oh."

"An unfortunate necessity," he said, sighing. "But it might be okay. I was thinking of getting meatballs and maybe a Poäng chair. They're more comfortable than you'd expect."

"They're..." I frowned. "You're going to IKEA?"

"We."

"What?"

"We're going to IKEA."

I almost laughed. "Oh, I'm invited?"

"Not at all. You're the purpose. We're getting a bed. And maybe a Poäng."

"What?" I said.

"A bed, Sean," he said patiently.

"I... okay."

Somehow, he knew what I was thinking.

"Don't overthink it, darling." He rotated his wrist, wincing as it cracked. "The bed is for me, because I've decided I want to stay here more often, but I'd also like to wake up in the morning without feeling like I have the back of an eighty-year-old. If you'd like to sleep in it when I'm not here, you're certainly welcome to."

I knew he was trying to be cute, but all it did was make me clench my jaw. Rick raised an eyebrow at my lack of response.

"What I mean is, I'll buy the bed if—"

"I don't need you to buy me anything," I said, trying to keep my voice steady. "I just never had a reason to get a bed, so I didn't. I don't need someone to take care of me or buy me shit because we hooked up or—"

"Sean." His voice was firm. "I'm not buying you shit because we hooked up and I'm not trying to take care of you. I mean, don't get me wrong, I'd love to take care of you, but I know you don't need that." He seemed to have regained feeling in his arm and reached forward, touching my cheek. "I want to be with you. I want us to be comfortable when we're together. And…"

He trailed off, a snickering sort of guilt in his eyes.

"Let me guess," I said tiredly. "Something, something, you like it rough."

He burst out laughing. "Not quite."

"What?"

He grinned wickedly. "When I said I liked it rough, I was talking about the sex, not about how your knees will feel after having to balance on this damn metal frame while you fuck me."

If it weren't for the fact that all the blood in my body seemed to concentrate in one place, I might have blushed.

"And it's in my best interest to make sure your knees stay healthy," he continued. "I mean, considering how good you look on them."

I swallowed hard as he licked his lips.

"Or, well, at least how good I *imagine* you look on them."

Fuck.

"And I mean, maybe a *little* bit of it is that I don't want my knees to hurt while I'm fucking you, since I fully plan on taking my time and—"

"For fuck's sake," I grumbled, and he was almost laughing too hard to kiss me back when I grabbed him.

Almost.

He was as hard as I was and his laughter turned to a groan as I pushed myself against him. There was a whirlpool of emotions still rushing through me—anger, embarrassment, desire, that almost unshakeable sense of being undeserving of Rick's attention—but it only took a moment before those all faded. I had to marvel at the way I could lose myself with him; nothing mattered but his lips and his body and his cock and the way his fingers traced along my ribs.

I shuddered as he grazed a particularly sensitive spot and Rick groaned again, thrusting his hips forward to grind his cock against me. As his head brushed my shaft, a trail of sticky wetness lingered, and I had to brace myself against him for a moment as I indulged in the sensation of his pre-cum dripping on me.

I needed more.

"On your back."

"Hmm?" he asked.

I pushed on his chest. "Get on your back."

He licked his lips and smirked, but rolled over as directed.

I don't think he expected me to push his legs open and settle between them so our cocks were pressed together, but he definitely didn't mind. He grinned as I adjusted, my balls resting against his as I lined our cocks up and wrapped my hands around them.

Around us.

He groaned a third time when I started moving, grinding myself against him, feeling each pulse and throb of his cock through my shaft. One of his hands ended up on my hip and the other clutched at the sheet as I moved faster, his eyes fluttering shut for a moment as his head tilted back.

"Fuck, Sean," he moaned. "That's... oh, God."

I smiled. I couldn't help it. When he opened his eyes and caught sight of it, he reached for me.

"Kiss me," he pleaded.

So of course I did.

I'd never gotten off quite like that. Rick held onto me fiercely as I kissed him, not letting me sit back up, so all I could do was grind my cock between our bodies. I had absolutely no complaint about that, and he didn't seem to either; he pushed his hips forward, grinding up until we found a rhythm that made my head spin. His arms were around my waist and his tongue was in my mouth and when he started panting, I knew he was close.

As eager as I was to come myself, I kept my pace steady. Well, I kept it as steady as I could with Rick grabbing at me, his fingers digging into my hips and ass as he lost himself to the sensation. He cried out and I knew, I *knew*, and I nipped at his lip as I started moving myself faster.

He came hard, ropes of cum spilling on his stomach and mine, and my movements meant that it started to smear between us. *That* was what I wanted, and what I needed, and I rubbed myself harder and faster as his cum coated our cocks.

When I came, I shuddered, my body jerking and light pulsing through my eyes as I erupted. I buried my face against Rick's neck and he held me, his breath soft and warm against my ear when I finally collapsed against him.

When I recovered enough to crawl off of Rick, I tried to get off the futon as carefully as I could so I wouldn't turn my sheets into a complete sticky mess. All was fine until I stood up and couldn't stop myself from grimacing.

"What's wrong?" Rick asked, concern in his eyes as he looked up at me.

"Nothing," I muttered.

"Sean."

"*Nothing*."

"Darling."

I sighed, then shook my head as I tried not to laugh. "That was a little hard on my knees."

He practically shot off the futon to tell me that he had, in fact, told me so, then bossily directed me to my bathroom so we could shower together before going to buy my new bed.

Twenty

THE SILVER LINING OF being frugal to the point of scantness was that I had a decent amount of money saved up.

It was hard for me to touch that money. Every purchase I made was weighed as to whether I could make do with what I had or do without. I'd gotten better, in recent months, at making sure I was spending a reasonable amount of money on what I deemed necessities. Once upon a time, I'd kept my apartment so cold that the landlord thought the furnace was broken and that I just hadn't noticed for some reason. It took Mario screaming at me for admitting I'd been living on plain white rice for most of my meals to start grocery shopping for proper food.

I was making progress. Slow progress, but progress.

At least, I was until that weekend with Rick, when I decided I was suddenly okay with spending a bunch of money on furnishing my apartment. I didn't want to consider what it said about me that one night with Rick was enough to turn that slow progress into an impulsive shopping trip to IKEA. Though, maybe it was less about me and more about my feelings for Rick.

And those feelings.

It felt like it was inevitable and a whirlwind at the same time. I'd known him, in a way, for months. He'd *known* me for far less time than that, yet of everyone in the world, he knew... well. This man, who was somehow still here, who somehow wanted to be here more often, so often that I was going to buy a fucking bed and a chair and who knew what else because I wanted him here, too, knew me as well as Mario. My best friend, the only person I trusted, the person who had been there at my lowest and helped me get to where I was, who I had known for *four years*, who was the family I'd chosen and who I loved completely.

Rick knew as much about me as Mario did.

Thinking about that was terrifying, so I ignored the implications and made coffee for the two of us after we showered.

I didn't own a car and was just going to get the mattress delivered, but Rick talked me into renting a truck so we could get the mattress home ourselves.

"Then you have it for tonight instead of having to wait for delivery."

I tried not to wonder if he was going to stay the night again. "And what if someone sees us?"

"Many people will see us. IKEA is usually busy."

I glared at him. "You know what I mean."

"I do, and I seriously have to wonder what the chances of seeing someone you know from work at IKEA is. You do *luxury* design."

It was a good point. "Fine. Okay."

He grinned, grabbed his phone, and started typing. "Let's see what we can get."

Both of us spent the next little while trying to track down a last-minute truck rental, but there didn't seem to be a single truck left in the city. Sighing, I put my phone down after being told no yet again.

"I'll just get it delivered," I said. "I can spend one more night on the futon."

"Not a chance," Rick said as he waited on hold with another company. "You either get a mattress today or you're spending the night at my place."

My mouth dropped open, but before I could respond, whoever was on the line with Rick picked up.

"Yep, still here!" he said, looking at me innocently. "Mm-hmm... yes, a pickup would be fine. It's just to get a mattress... the afternoon, maybe? We can have it back tonight..." He grinned and cradled the phone on his shoulder, digging in his pocket. "Yep, we'll take it. Just let me grab my card."

"Use mine," I said insistently, grabbing my wallet and pulling my credit card out.

He didn't argue as he took it and booked the truck, thanking the person profusely. When he hung up, there was a self-satisfied smirk on his face.

"We can pick it up in an hour," he said, ignoring my outstretched hand and instead reaching across the table to grab my wallet. "As long as we have it back before they close tonight, everything should be fine. Just have to fill it up and—oh, I don't want to scratch this."

I felt the blood drain from my face. "Wait, I—"

But it was too late. He'd seen the edge of the picture I'd forgotten was in my wallet, and he'd pulled it out from the spot I'd tucked it safely away, and he was looking at it.

The man had seen me cry multiple times. He'd seen me at my worst. He'd had my cock in his mouth and made me come—twice, he had seen me at my most vulnerable. He had rubbed his cock against me and tasted me and kissed me and touched me intimately.

And yet, it wasn't until he was looking at the photo of my family that I truly felt naked.

"Is this them?" he asked unnecessarily.

I didn't respond, which clearly meant yes.

"I'm sorry," he said, also unnecessarily because, strangely enough, I wasn't mad. "But also, oh my *God* were you an adorable kid."

"What happened, am I right?" I muttered, and he laughed.

I sighed and held my hand out, and this time he obediently handed me the item I was reaching for. Glancing down at the photo brought that familiar surge of anger as I looked at my dad, the heartbreaking frustration and betrayal as I looked at my mom, the overwhelming guilt as I looked at my sister, and the hatred as I looked at myself.

"I don't know why I keep it."

"Because they're your family," he replied. "Because as hard as it is, that won't change."

I snorted softly. "It just pisses me off."

"What does?"

"Seeing them. I hate it."

I felt Rick studying me from across the table, but I couldn't bring myself to look up at him.

"Why?" he asked.

"You wouldn't understand."

"Probably not," he admitted. "I know I've been lucky. But I'd like to try to understand."

I pressed my lips together, then put the photo on the table.

"Disowned me. Told me to kill myself." I tapped on my dad's face.

"Let him kick me out. Picked him over me." I tapped on my mom's face.

"Left her with her abusive prick of a father and a mother who's not going to protect her." Lacey's face.

Then, my face. I smiled wryly.

"This one was just made wrong."

"He most certainly was not," Rick said.

I shrugged and stood up suddenly, bringing the photo to the fridge and tucking it under a magnet.

"Sean," Rick said. "You were not made wrong."

"We need to go pick up the truck," I said.

He got up and strode across the kitchen, pulling me into his arms. "You were *not* made wrong."

"Okay."

He touched my chin, tilting my head up, then moved his fingers to the cross around my neck. "I think you wear this for the same reason you keep that photo."

I raised my eyebrows. "Do you?"

"You said it yourself. It pisses you off."

"And you think I like being pissed off?" I asked flatly.

"I think you use it to remind yourself of how much you've been hurt in the past," he said. "Because you think if you forget how to be angry, something bad will happen again."

I scoffed. "Sure. That makes sense."

"It does."

"What am I supposed to do? Just forgive and forget?"

He shrugged and I gaped at him.

"Are you fucking kidding? After everything—"

"Is your anger hurting them? Or is it just hurting you?"

I opened my mouth to snap back at him, to tell him it was none of his business, that he didn't understand, that he would *never* understand, but nothing came out.

"I mean, if you want to be chained to your anger your entire life, then don't." Rick hugged me closer. "But if you want freedom from your past, forgiving yourself would be a good step towards that."

Somehow, I couldn't bring myself to argue with him.

Somehow, I started to think that maybe he was right.

"I like you the way you are. Don't think for a second that I don't, okay?" His lips brushed the side of my head. "You have every right to be angry about what happened to you. But you also have every right to be happy. You *deserve* happiness, okay?"

"I..." I tried to find my voice, but it wavered and cracked.

"I know. You don't believe it. But I'm going to keep saying it until you believe it, whether that happens because it's true or because you're tired of hearing me gush about how amazing you are and believe it out of exasperation."

I laughed and he kissed the side of my head again, then reluctantly let go of me.

"Now, enough reliving your sad memories, darling. We have a bed to buy. And maybe a Poäng. And perhaps a Lack table." He tapped a finger to his chin. "How do you feel about red accents?"

When he looked back at me, I had my arms folded and was trying to look at him pointedly, but the ridiculous sparkle in his eyes just made me laugh.

Twenty-One

God works in mysterious ways.

That's the cliche, isn't it? Whenever something bad happens, it's God working in a mysterious way. My parents said it all the time while I was growing up. When the car broke down on the way to church and we were stranded on the side of the road, only to find a small bird that Lacey and I nursed back to health, that was Him working in a mysterious way. When a little girl who lived three blocks away from us was paralyzed from the waist down after being hit by a car while walking home from school, it wasn't up to us to question His ways. There was some lesson He was trying to teach, my dad said. There was some purpose He needed her to fulfill that she could only do after experiencing hardship. It was either that or she was being punished for sinning.

For some reason, her parents didn't find that especially comforting.

As it stood, I didn't know how much of that I believed. In my experience, God's ways weren't all that mysterious. I tended to think He operated under more of a "fuck that guy in particular" sort of way, where "that guy" was me and "fuck" was just punishment after punishment for being created by His enemy. At face value, there was no mystery in that.

At the same time, mysterious ways brought Rick into my life. Mysterious ways kept him there. I don't know whose mysterious ways they were; I didn't expect anything but misery from God, and I still didn't understand what Rick saw in me, but I wasn't about to complain.

He offered to drive when we picked up the rental truck, but I shook my head. As much as I appreciated the offer, I wasn't quite there yet. No one did things for me; I'd been responsible for myself for so long that the fact he even wanted to be with me felt like too much. Maybe one day I'd be more comfortable accepting the things he so desperately wanted to give, but that day, I was already pushing the line of what I could handle.

IKEA was busy, because of course it was. It was a Saturday afternoon and half of Montreal seemed to be in the store. The parking lot wasn't full, at least, though Rick laughed at me when I parked about as far away from the store as I could.

"I'm not used to driving a big vehicle," I grumbled as he hopped out of the truck.

He shut the door with his hip and walked around the truck, laughter still crinkling the corner of his eyes.

"Of course you're not, darling." My heart fluttered as he took my hand boldly. "It's not like you've ever had to overcompensate for something."

My face went red and that just made him laugh more. I let him think it was because of his dick joke and not the fact that he was the first person I'd ever held hands with in public like that. I'd danced with guys at the gay bar, sure, and I'd been on a couple of dates, but holding hands with someone as we casually strolled across the parking lot?

My heart was on fire.

Part of me waited for someone to comment on the fact that we were shoving our sexuality in their faces or scoff at the bold display of two men shopping on a Saturday afternoon, but it never came. The only comment I heard was from a lady with a thick Quebecois accent who looked to be in her eighties. She smiled as Rick and I approached the entrance and nudged the much-younger woman with her.

"Look at those boys! How sweet!" she said in French, her voice a whisper that was not any lower in volume than the buzz of conversation around us.

"Mémé!" the younger woman admonished, looking at us apologetically.

Rick smiled that easy, gorgeous, winning smile first at her, then at the older woman, and squeezed my hand.

"Better than the alternative," he said softly.

"Have you heard the alternative often?"

"Of course." He squeezed my hand again. "Not going to let it stop me from showing off the hot piece I've got on my arm, though."

My face burned again and he snickered as we entered the store.

I'd like to say it took longer than expected to get to the bed frames and mattresses, but that would be a lie. I fully expected Rick to get distracted every three feet and insist on touring each of the showrooms, which he absolutely did.

"See?" he said at one point, folding himself into a chair with a red cushion. "Poäng. It's so comfortable."

"And why do I need a Poäng?" I asked tiredly.

"Because I'd like to have somewhere comfortable to sit when I'm at your place," he said in a tone that mocked mine.

"Why can't we just sit on the futon?"

He raised an eyebrow at me.

"It's not that bad!" I protested.

"Trust me, you want this chair." He stood and motioned at it. "Try it. Seriously."

I obliged and sat in the chair, which was as comfortable as he claimed it was, but still shook my head.

"Why not?" he huffed as I stood up.

"Why would I need it?"

"I'll give you a lap dance in it."

I nearly gave myself whiplash as I looked around to see if anyone had heard him. When I looked back at Rick, he was grinning.

"So the red cushion is fine?"

"Yes," I grumbled, but I couldn't quite hold my smile back as he wrapped an arm around my shoulders and led me to the next showroom.

He managed to talk me into a coffee table and a nightstand, but I put my foot down when it came to adding a desk and swivel chair.

"I can work at the kitchen table," I said firmly. "I don't need this right now."

Still, when we finally got to the beds and mattresses, I had a list that was a fair bit longer than what I'd originally intended. I thought I'd mind a little more, but as Rick took my hand and tugged me towards the rows of test mattresses, I found I really didn't.

"I'm not getting a king-size mattress," I said as he beelined to the nearest one.

He gasped in mock horror. "But—"

"I don't have *room* for that."

He sighed dramatically as he sat down. "I guess I can settle for a queen."

"I was thinking a double."

"Sean, no. A queen."

I sighed. "A double is *fine*. It's less expensive and…"

Before I finished, he got off the king-size mattress, looked at me pointedly, and found the nearest double. Without so much as a second glance at me, he got onto the mattress.

"I will buy it for you myself, I swear to God," he threatened, then laid on his back.

I burst out laughing. I couldn't help it; even with his head nearly at the edge of the mattress, his feet were hanging off the bottom. He turned his head towards me and grinned, tapping his toes together before sitting back up.

"Okay," I said. "Fair. I'll get a queen."

"That'll do." He stood up. "It works out, anyway. I've already got a king."

"Do you?"

"Of course." He took my hand and led me down the row of beds. "I've got you."

I groaned, but that was just to cover the sound of the butterflies in my stomach.

Begrudgingly, I laid down on every queen-sized mattress in the showroom since Rick insisted I couldn't just pick one at random.

"This is stupid," I complained as I lay on my back under his watchful eye. "I've been sleeping on a *futon*. They all feel like good beds to me."

"You must have a preference," he argued.

"I don't even know what the difference is!"

"They have different firmness levels. Do you like the softer ones?" He licked his lips and grinned wickedly.

"Don't," I said, but I was already laughing.

"I mean, if you like it harder, you know I'm not going to complain."

I shook my head as I got off the mattress. "This one feels pretty good, I guess. What do you think?"

Before he could try it out, my world crumbled.

"Sean?" said a voice from behind me.

Of all the people I expected to see strolling through an IKEA looking for modern but affordable flatpack furniture, my boss was not one of them.

"Rick," Leanne continued as all the blood drained from my face. "A pleasure to see you."

"And you, Leanne," Rick said, his easy-going tone far more forced than usual.

She turned to me, her face neutral. "This is a surprise."

My heart thudded painfully in my chest, my pulse so loud I could barely think.

"I... yeah," I said quietly.

"How long has this been going on?"

"A day," Rick said sharply. "Literally."

She looked vaguely amused. "And you, what, brought a U-haul to your second date?"

I felt like I was going to puke.

"It's a bit more complicated than that," Rick said evenly.

She stared at him for a moment before turning back to me. "How long has this really been going on?"

"We went out last night," I answered softly. "Other than that, just... just through work."

"And is that why the project was delayed?"

I shook my head. "I didn't—"

"That wasn't on him," Rick said. "I was the one making the changes so I could see him. And Theo and Aspen know that. I told them."

Leanne didn't look at him. "You're aware of the company's policy?"

"May I also remind you I'm not technically a client of your firm?" Rick said loudly.

"I'm quite aware of your role, Mr. McDougall," she said sharply. "Thank you."

Rick fell silent and Leanne turned back to me.

"You're aware of the policy about relationships with clients?"

I nodded, staring at the ground just past Leanne's left arm. At least I wouldn't have to go into the office to be fired. Monique would pack up my personal items on Monday and they'd be sent to my apartment, which I'd have until the end of the month to vacate since I wouldn't be able to pay my rent without a job, but at least I'd be there long enough to get the package and—

"I'm going to let you in on a secret," she said. "On the condition that you never, *ever* repeat it in the office."

I looked up, confused.

"I'm the reason for that policy."

To say I was shocked was an understatement. If I didn't know better, I'd say there was amusement behind that stony expression, but she looked away from me and smiled.

"Yes, come meet Sean," she said, and I turned to see a short woman who looked slightly younger than Leanne walking towards us.

Leanne was the epitome of businesslike. She had stylishly short hair and wore impeccable skirt suits that demanded respect. Even on the weekend, she was dressed in a way that wouldn't have been out of place in an office. The woman who approached us was nearly a polar opposite: her hair was dyed jet-black and hung around her shoulders. She had a pierced septum and wore a flowy black shirt over jeans.

"Sean, this is my wife, Nina," Leanne said. "Nina, one of my newer associates, Sean Lemieux."

"Oooh!" squealed Nina, doing a strange jig as she bounded beside Leanne before thrusting her hand forward so I could shake it. "I can't believe I get to meet one of your work people!"

The corners of Leanne's mouth flicked up as she turned back to me. "Nina was a client of ours a number of years ago, long before I took over managing the firm."

"I was a fan of the full service package," Nina giggled.

Leanne rolled her eyes.

"The point, Sean, is that I realize this may be one of those... circumstances," she said. "With anyone else on the team, I'd be exceptionally concerned about discovering this. With you two..." She looked from me to Rick and then back to me. "He is not *technically* a client, which means you have done nothing against policy. I have no concerns whatsoever that this will cause any issues—any *additional* issues that have not already been addressed—with the project."

"It won't," I promised.

"I would strongly suggest you not parade this information around the firm, at least until the project is complete," she continued. "I've had to slap Vincent on the wrist a couple of times for similar behaviour and, selfishly, I don't want to have another meeting with him about how unfair he thinks I am."

"I mean, it is a little unfair," Nina said. "You're giving Sean preferential treatment."

"Well, I like Sean more than I like Vincent," Leanne replied patiently. "So yes, I'm going to be a bad manager and allow him to break a rule he's not actually breaking in the first place because I trust he won't let it affect his work performance."

"And also because you two look so cute together," Nina said, winking at me.

"That's very true," Rick agreed. "We are adorable."

My face went red as Nina laughed.

"Be that as it may," Leanne continued, turning to him. "Rick, that policy is in place as much to protect my employees as it is to protect our clients. Do you understand?"

"Take good care of Sean, got it." He smiled and took my hand. "I will *gladly* do that. Do I have to submit a weekly report to you or...?"

"Please don't," I whispered as Leanne started laughing.

When they walked away a few minutes later, I sat down on the nearest mattress and took a deep breath. Rick settled beside me, grinning.

"Well Sean, darling, I—"

"Don't say you told me so," I said. "You couldn't have ever guessed that would happen. That was a fucking coincidence of divine proportions."

"What's that saying?" he asked idly. "God works in mysterious ways?"

I snorted, a tickle of emotion starting in my nose. I blinked hard, not sure why I felt like crying, and his thumb moved against mine.

I was relieved, more than anything, but the disbelief was intense. In my mind, it was nothing short of a miracle. Who had decided I was worthy of a miracle and why was beyond me. Who would have decided that I was allowed to be happy? That I was allowed to be with Rick and keep my job and feel whole again? And why now?

It didn't matter, though. Not really. My heart had gone through a whirlwind of emotions: fear, shame, panic, predictable resignation at something I'd somehow been certain would happen, despite its unlikeliness. A warm feeling of encouragement, surprisingly enough. I felt cared for and supported and appreciated.

Above all, I felt something I used to dread. Something that was becoming part of me, something that Rick had put there and that wasn't fading. Something that meant things were changing. That maybe, just maybe, Rick was right, and I deserved to be happy, and I deserved to be comfortable, and I deserved to be safe.

Maybe God was working in mysterious ways so I could literally see that it was okay to have hope again.

Twenty-Two

ONE FUTON IN THE folded-up position.

A dark wood bed frame with a queen-size mattress and box spring.

New bed sheets—white—and a new bedspread—red, with a subtle herringbone pattern.

Four new pillows, plus two throw pillows Rick insisted I *had* to have.

A Poäng chair with a red cushion and matching ottoman.

A coffee table, two nightstands, and a bookshelf. A throw blanket for the back of the futon. A new set of plates, cups, bowls, and cutlery. Another frying pan and a set of not-great-but-good-enough kitchen knives. One potted plant.

And the one thing I let Rick pay for: a silly print of two coffee cups sitting on a reddish-brown table that he insisted was *not* mahogany.

We brought my new things in together, then brought the rental truck back after making a quick detour to Rick's place so he could grab some clean clothes. When we returned, Rick helped me build the bedframe and put the mattress and box spring on it. While I put the coffee table and the fucking Poäng chair together, he hung the print he'd got me, then put away the various sundry items we'd purchased. Once the new sheets and blankets had been washed and dried, we made the bed together.

I knew it would make a difference aesthetically. What I didn't expect was how I would feel when I stepped back and looked around at the room I'd lived in for years. It felt brand new. It felt... warm.

With Rick standing in the middle of it, it felt like home.

He turned in place, examining every change we'd made, before looking back at me with his hands on his hips.

"Look at what a difference a new mattress makes," he said, grinning.

"Oh, of course," I said, rolling my eyes. "This is entirely due to the new mattress."

"Why, has anything else changed?"

"You're a dork."

I didn't know what the future held for me and Rick. I knew what I wanted it to hold, but at that moment, I was still uncertain I even deserved him. But in my mind, what I wanted was clear.

I wanted to see him laugh the way he did after I called him a dork. Every day, if I could. I wanted to see the corners of his eyes crinkle as he howled, then admonished me. I wanted more trips to IKEA. More trips anywhere, really. The grocery store, the coffee shop, a stroll through a park; it didn't matter where. I just wanted more time with him. More days holding his hand and more breathless kisses and more whispered jokes that made my face turn red. I wanted more nights out with my friends—our friends, if he wanted—and more mornings waking up in his arms.

And, for some reason, he wanted me, too.

Once he finished laughing, he decided we were getting dinner delivered and that we were having Chinese. While he ordered, I took a quick shower, since I was fairly sweaty after putting all the furniture together.

Plus, he'd hinted that we might... well.

I didn't know if Rick was the type of guy who was particular about "cleaning up" before sex. I wasn't. Things should be *clean*, obviously, but I wasn't into not eating all day or following a strict diet or anything like I knew some guys were. It was about fifty-fifty with my friends; I knew Armand didn't care either way when he was topping but that Breton had a very particular routine he followed. But I didn't know what Rick's feelings were on the subject. If he cared, that was fine. We just wouldn't go there tonight. But if he didn't, I wanted to be ready for him. Because I wanted it.

I wanted him.

Dinner arrived and we ate, Rick making fun of me for not knowing how to use chopsticks and me rolling my eyes as he ate his chicken fried rice painfully slowly. He'd ordered way too much food, of course, and he insisted it wasn't on purpose even though there was enough left over to feed me for two or three days. I pretended I believed him.

"Help me pack this up," he said as he started clearing the table. "We can have leftovers for lunch tomorrow but you'll need to finish the rest of it this week since we have dinner plans."

"Do we?" I asked, stacking some of the containers together.

"Mm-hmm. I'm taking you on our first real date." He stacked our plates together and brought them to the sink. "We also should reschedule drinks with Mario and your friends. They didn't *really* get a chance to get to know me, which just isn't fair to them."

"Because you're so amazing?"

"Because I'm so amazing."

I laughed and went to open the fridge, hesitating as I saw the picture of my family I'd put there that morning.

I don't know why I'd put it there. I hadn't thought about it; I'd just wanted to stop talking about it and that seemed like the natural place to put it. Looking at it stirred up that familiar feeling, but it also stirred up something... something. I didn't know what.

All I knew is that I looked at my dad and at the coldness in his eyes. Even from a photo taken provinces away and years long past, I felt like he was glaring his disapproval through the lens of the camera. Like he was watching, like he still saw the evil that was me, like he could see me sinning with my...

"Are you my boyfriend?" I asked without thinking, then cringed at how needy it sounded. "I mean—"

"Yep," Rick said. "I meant to tell you earlier but I forgot. You're *my* boyfriend so that makes me *your* boyfriend."

My boyfriend.

I stared at my dad's face, frowning. If I was sinning with Rick, that made Rick a sinner by association. But Rick... he wasn't. I refused to believe for a second that someone as kind and generous as him was a sinner. There was nothing wrong with who he was or how he lived. He'd been made a certain way and he couldn't change that anymore than I could. And if that didn't make him a sinner—if he wasn't made by the devil—then why did that make *me* a sinner?

"Sean?"

I jumped as he came up behind me.

"What's wrong?" he asked.

"Nothing."

He looked at the photo, then took the containers of leftovers from me and put them away. When he closed the fridge again, I reached forward and slipped the magnet over my dad's face.

"You okay?" Rick asked.

I looked at him and smiled. "Yeah."

"Whew. I was starting to worry, seeing as you threw out the whole 'are you my boyfriend' thing and then went silent when I confirmed that I was."

I grimaced. "Sorry. I was—"

"Thinking, I know." He guided me so my back was to the fridge and kissed me gently. "You think too much."

"One of us has to."

He laughed as he kissed me again, lingering a bit longer that time.

"Are you okay with that?" he asked after we parted. "Being... like, together?"

I nodded. "If you are."

"Why wouldn't I be?"

I bit my lip, looking up at him nervously. "You just... you know."

He raised his eyebrow and I took a breath.

"When we first met, you talked about not wanting to settle down. You said—"

"That I used to worry if I settled down with someone, I might've missed the right one," he finished, then grinned. "That flew right over your head."

"What did?"

"The hint."

"What hint?" I asked indignantly.

"Used to,'" he said. "As in, past tense. As in, I was pretty sure I'd found a nice guy I wanted to settle down with."

I blinked, the sudden realization washing over me.

"It was you, for the record," he continued. "Just in case that wasn't—"

"Yeah, I got it," I said, laughing.

He brushed my hair back. "Does it bother you?"

"What?"

"That I used to get around a bit."

I shook my head. "Does it bother you that you're technically my first boyfriend?"

"Not even a little." He kissed me, nipping at my lip. "It means you don't have any horrible bad habits I have to break. Have I mentioned it's tradition to give your boyfriend a massage after you insist on dragging him to IKEA and only let him buy *one* silly little piece of wall art?"

"Asshole," I muttered, and I felt him grin.

That kiss lingered, as did the next one. On the one after that, Rick moved a little closer and I rested my arms on his shoulders, and on the one after *that*, he nudged me until my back was pressed firmly against the fridge.

"How are your knees feeling?" he murmured.

I smiled, still kissing him. "Mmm, a little rough after this morning. Maybe you should be the one to test your knees on the mattress."

Something between a laugh and a groan vibrated against my mouth. "So that's what you were doing in the shower."

"What?" I asked innocently.

His teeth grazed along my lip. "Getting all nice and clean for me?"

"Maybe. Unless you prefer, like... uh..."

"A shower is perfectly fine by me," he murmured. "What about you?"

I gasped slightly as he nipped at my lip. "Same."

He chuckled again. "You have condoms?"

"Mm-hmm."

"Lube?"

"Of course."

He groaned again and his hands moved along my sides, from my hips up to my ribs, then wrapped around my waist as he deepened the kiss.

For a bit longer, he kissed me and touched me and nuzzled against me. His head dipped down and he kissed my neck, teeth scraping lightly against my collarbone. I rested against the fridge, my head tilted back and my hands on his broad shoulders as he sucked on my neck, just enough that I was fairly certain he'd left a mark.

I didn't mind that at *all*, if the way my cock reacted was any indication.

He felt me get harder and harder, his bulge becoming more prominent as mine did. Just when I thought I couldn't take it anymore, he moved his lips from my neck back to my lips and kissed me before pulling away.

"Bed," he said.

"Yes, I have one now."

He snickered. "Go get on it, you dork."

I laughed, grabbing a towel to bring along with us before we crossed my apartment to the bed. Despite telling me to get on it, Rick stopped me so he could undress me, and it only made sense for me to do the same to him. Piece by piece, I revealed him as he revealed me, stopping to admire him only once every stitch of clothing was on the ground.

He didn't let me admire him for long; once I was naked, he took me in his arms again and pulled me onto the bed. Our lips connected as we flopped onto the bedspread, hands busily exploring each other as the heat between us sparked and flared and grew. I couldn't stop myself from pressing against him, determined to feel every inch of skin against mine at once if I could. He certainly didn't seem to mind, aiding me in my pursuit as he ground his cock against me.

Pre-cum was already leaking from him, sticky and warm against my skin. I reached down and wrapped my fingers around him, eliciting another one of those perfect, musical groans as I slowly stroked his cock. He let a kiss linger against my lips for a long, amazing moment before reluctantly drawing himself away.

"Lube is where?" he asked.

I rolled over and grabbed the lube and a condom. Rick took them from me, then nuzzled against my shoulder before directing me on my knees. I couldn't stop myself from shivering as he moved behind me, his hands trailing down my back and to my ass.

He caressed me with featherlight touches, his fingers seeming to savour me as he traced little patterns along my skin. I jumped a bit when he pressed a kiss against the small of my back, not expecting to feel the softness of his mouth, but relaxed as he trailed his fingers along my crack.

I let out a soft exhale as the tip of one finger found my hole and teased it. He played there for a moment before reaching down to cup my balls, making me groan as he fondled them. When he pulled his hands away, there was a flutter of disappointment, but the sound of him opening the lube quashed that *very* quickly.

He used one hand to spread my ass and I tensed in anticipation, waiting for the momentary shock of cold. When it didn't come, I bit my lip, then twisted so I could look at Rick. He caught my eye and smiled, then his finger returned to my hole. I jumped just a little when the cool gel met my skin, then moaned softly as the tip of Rick's finger pushed inside me. Still he held my gaze, his eyes captivating me until I couldn't handle it any longer. My eyes fluttered shut as he thrust more of his finger inside my ass.

I groaned as he pulled his finger out. Maybe he was taking pity on me or maybe he was as eager as I was, but he didn't hesitate before letting it sink back in. Carefully, he fingered me, exploring my hole with one hand as the other squeezed my hip. I gripped the bedspread, barely able to stop myself from pushing back against him. When he finally added a second finger, I was in a mindless haze, controlled only by how much I wanted him.

And it must have been obvious that I wanted him a lot. His movements grew quicker, firmer, stretching me around his fingers and making my cock throb. As he fingered me, his other hand left my hip, slipping to the front of my body so he could wrap his fingers around my cock.

It was heaven.

It was fucking *heaven*.

"Please," I groaned as he started stroking me.

"Please what?" came the amused reply.

I had no idea what I was pleading for. I wanted more, wanted him, wanted everything all at once. There wasn't an easy way to say that, though, and being a bit distracted, all I could do was bury my face against the bedspread.

"Please," I said again, and he laughed before pulling his fingers out of my ass and letting go of my cock.

He pressed a soft kiss against my back again and I opened my eyes when I heard the crinkle of the condom wrapper. Twisting, I watched as he unrolled it. When he realized I was watching him, he smiled, then moved forward to kiss me.

"What do you want?" he asked again. "I wanna hear you say it."

Oh, God.

"I want your cock," I murmured.

The noise he made was so indecent that if I weren't already on my knees, it would have brought me to them.

He moved behind me and opened the lube again. Moments later, both hands were spreading me open, and I felt the gentle nudge of his head against my hole.

"Ready?" he asked, his voice dripping with lust.

"Yes," I groaned. "*Please.*"

He groaned, one hand moved from my ass to my hip and the other to his cock, and then he pushed forward.

The bedspread was balled up in my fist as the head of his cock slipped inside me. I moaned as the thickness of his cock practically split me open, feeling every single inch he was giving me. Both his hands ended up on my hips and gripped hard as he sank into me, guiding my body back even as he moved forward. The sensation was intense, both painful and not as my hole stretched around him. I held my breath, my eyes slammed shut until his balls brushed against mine and his hips met my ass.

"Oh my God," he groaned. "Fuck, Sean."

"Please," I said again, and pushed back against him.

The grip on my hips tightened, he pulled out, and then he absolutely obliged me.

It wasn't my first time, but it was my best time. Hands down, there was nothing that compared to Rick. He fucked me hard, but he fucked me *good*, making sure the entire time that it felt as good for me as I assumed it did for him. I was gasping for breath, the entirety of my being consumed by the feel of him, the way he filled me, and the throbbing of my own cock.

And then, while he was fully inside me, he paused for a moment. The angle of his cock changed ever so slightly and his lips pressed against the base of my neck. A hand slid around my body, fingers trailing along my stomach, and then he grabbed my cock.

I was lost.

He was hitting the *perfect* spot. My body was on fire, every nerve inside me tingling as his cock passed over my prostate. And to stroke my cock at the same time, his arm wrapped around me as he controlled every bit of my pleasure? I was fucking *his*, completely and entirely. It was all I could do to hold onto the bed so I didn't float away. Nothing existed but me and him and complete bliss. I had no body; I was built of nothing but sensations and pleasure wrapped around a man who knew how broken I was and still wanted me.

He was everything.

I couldn't hold on very long after he started stroking me. It was too much to have him inside me and around me, behind me and in front of me, consuming me and completing me. My vision blurred; whether it was my senses or my emotions that were overwhelmed, I didn't know. Likely both, and I didn't mind in the slightest.

I moaned his name again and heard him swear. Fire burned inside me, a spark that became a roar, something I was chasing and yet running from until I simply couldn't any longer and gave into the pleasure threatening to seize me. My orgasm *ripped* through me, tearing my mind from my soul from my body from reality. I couldn't see; I couldn't hear; all I could do was feel the thickness of Rick's cock inside me and the distinct sensation that I was erupting. Every muscle in my body clenched as I shot load after load. It was so intense and drawn out that I didn't think I was ever going to *stop* coming and for a second, for a brief but very real second, I was fairly certain I'd ceased to exist at all.

Never before had I come so hard I'd had a fucking existential crisis.

Slowly, though, the atoms and molecules that made up my cells reformed, and the pieces of me came back together, and there was a heavy weight resting against my back that I assumed meant Rick had finished at some point while I was stuck between the planes of existence. Beneath me, the towel I'd thankfully remembered to grab was a complete wreck, and I couldn't stop myself from laughing as I realized it.

"Oh good," Rick said. "You're okay."

That just made me laugh harder.

He pulled out and helped guide me away from the mess I'd made beneath us, cradling me in his arms as I tried to remember how to use words.

"Wow," I finally said, and he pressed a kiss to my forehead.

"You were amazing," he whispered.

"You were..." I shook my head. "Never leave me, please."

It came out without my permission; the words hadn't even formed in my mind before I was saying them. I realized far too late what it sounded like. My eyes flew open as I panicked, mentally kicking myself for sounding too desperate, too pushy, too pathetic. He was my first boyfriend. He'd been my boyfriend for a *day*.

But before I could say anything else, Rick pulled me in for a kiss.

"How could I ever leave you?" he murmured comfortingly, blue eyes sparkling as they met mine. "You were made for me, darling."

Epilogue

I CLEARED MY THROAT as the car pulled into the driveway. Leanne glanced at me sidelong.

"Nervous?"

"Yep," I said.

She let out a soft snort that I'd learned was her version of a chuckle. "At least it's people you know. That has to make it easier."

"Maybe if it was anyone besides Aspen. She's terrifying."

Leanne snorted again, but there wasn't enough time for her to respond before three of the car doors opened.

From the backseat came Theo, looking as stylishly disheveled as ever. On the passenger side, the aforementioned Aspen, as beautiful as she was intimidating.

And from the driver's side, looking as delicious as he had when I'd kissed him goodbye before leaving my apartment that morning, came Rick.

"Hey, Sean!" called Theo as he walked towards the house. "Leanne! What a surprise. I didn't expect you to be here for the walkthrough."

"I hope you don't mind," she said. "This is Sean's first official walkthrough as a lead, so I thought it would be good for me to observe."

"Not at all," said Aspen, trying to smile what I think was intended to be a calming smile but just made my stomach curl all over again. "It's good to see you again."

"Leanne, am I allowed to treat him like my boyfriend if you're the only other employee around?" Rick asked.

Aspen and Theo laughed as my face went red.

Leanne smiled. "Considering it's the final task of the project, I think we can allow it."

"Thank God." Rick kissed me quickly and wrapped an arm around my shoulder. "Well, darling, shall we show them the house we designed?"

I tried not to laugh. "I'll walk them through the house I designed, sure."

The final walkthrough was straightforward enough. Technically, it was supposed to give the client the chance to review the work and make sure it was all to their liking. In actuality, it was simply an opportunity for us to show off the final product. By the time the walkthrough took place, all the little things that needed fixing or adjusting had happened; there was no reason that something surprising would happen while on it.

That day was no exception. Theo and Aspen had already seen the interior; aside from a few rooms that needed painting, nothing had changed since the last time they'd been there. Still, I went through the entire list to the letter as they patiently watched the pageantry put on for Leanne's benefit.

As hard as it was for me to brag, it *was* a beautiful home. I knew every inch of that place better than I knew my own apartment; I'd designed it and redesigned it so many times that I could have wandered the floor plan walking backwards with my eyes closed. Still, I couldn't help but be nervous. It was like waiting on a final judgement of whether I'd passed or failed.

When we finished the tour and returned to the front door, I looked nervously at Rick, then at Aspen.

"Any questions?" I asked her, then remembered it was also Theo's house and looked at him.

"Not from me," he said.

Aspen studied the house for a painfully long moment before looking at me. "No questions, just a comment."

Oh, God.

"Yes?" I asked.

"You did a fantastic job, even though you had to work with Rick."

"Hey!" Rick said indignantly as Theo burst out laughing.

I grinned. "It was a challenge, but I managed somehow."

"Sean!" Leanne admonished, but she and Aspen had both started laughing.

"What?" I said innocently. "I can say that. He's not a client."

He bumped me with his hip, but smiled.

For a few more minutes, we stood on the front step of Theo and Aspen's house talking and laughing. I'd gotten to know them better in the months since construction on their house had started. Rick had insisted on bringing me by for dinner within a week of us deciding we were a couple.

"You have Mario," he'd said. "And I have Theo. Getting along with him is non-negotiable."

Luckily, it was not a problem at all. Theo was probably the most easygoing guy I'd ever met. I still didn't quite understand how he and Aspen made things work—I wasn't entirely joking, she *did* terrify me a bit—but considering he was a literal rock star, his laid-back attitude seemed surprising. Still, they were happy, and they were happy for Rick, and they seemed to like me now that they knew I hadn't spent months trying to sneakily make them spend more money on their house.

"Well, then," Leanne said. "It seems like this is it. Sean, do you have the final paperwork?"

I nodded and pulled it out of my notebook, handing it to Aspen. "Once you sign here, that's it. Project done."

It was bittersweet. On one hand, finishing the project meant that I didn't have to hide my relationship with Rick at work. Not that it took much effort, but I kind of wanted to put a picture of us up at my desk and until the project was officially finished, I couldn't do that.

On the other, it meant that my weekly "meetings" with Rick were over. Sure, I could just go out for lunch with him or something, but it wasn't quite the same as sneaking kisses in the meeting room.

Still, all things had to come to an end, and after reading the paperwork, Aspen signed it without question.

"That's it, then," she said, handing it back to me.

"It's been a pleasure," I said earnestly.

"Literally," Rick said, and Theo snickered.

I smiled and tucked the paperwork into my notebook.

"Well, should we head back to the office?" Leanne asked, even though it clearly wasn't a question.

"Probably." I nodded at Theo and Aspen. "Thank you both."

"Anytime," Theo said.

"But not really," Aspen added. "We're not building another house anytime soon."

I laughed and turned to Rick. "See you tonight?"

"Actually," Rick said. "Before you go…"

I raised my eyebrows and he grinned.

"I was wondering what I have to do to get a meeting for a consultation."

"What?" I asked.

"I mean, you did *such* a good job on this house. I'm sure you're looking for another project to take on. Maybe you can design one for me now."

"You can't be serious," I said, trying not to laugh.

He was, though. He was very serious, and nearly a year to the day later, we had the final walkthrough for Rick's project.

The house I'd designed for Theo and Aspen was beautiful. The one I designed for Rick, though?

It was everything.

On the outside, it seemed small and unassuming. On the inside, the hardwood floors gleamed and the railings had intricate patterns carved into them. The kitchen was bright and open with a door leading out to a roomy deck. Upstairs, the master bedroom had a bathroom that was the *epitome* of luxury: two sinks, an oversized shower, and a soaker tub big enough for a six-foot-four man and possibly his boyfriend to sit together.

The walkthrough was pointless; Rick had seen it all before. We went through the charade, though, and he pretended to be very interested as I pointed out the things I *told* him would look better than the inane ideas he'd had.

"I suppose you were right," he said as we finished and returned to the front hallway. "The bathroom looks far better with marble instead of granite."

"Told you so," I muttered.

"There's just one more thing," he said.

I knew what he was about to say. I mean, we'd talked about it. I'd all but started packing. Hell, from the moment the project had started, it hadn't just been *his* house. He'd acted completely different from when we were designing Theo and Aspen's place; more often than not, he told me to do whatever I wanted, and construction on his project started far more quickly than it had on Theo and Aspen's.

Still, my stomach flipped as I looked up, and up, and *up* at him, feeling as small and safe as I had since the first day we'd been together.

"What's that?" I asked.

"It's a little big for one person."

"Are you asking me to move in with you?"

He touched the side of my face and leaned in, his lips brushing mine. "So what if I am?"

I smiled against his mouth.

"I'd say it would be a dream come true."

Acknowledgments

My books would not be possible without some very special people:

My proof-readers, editors, and beta readers are extraordinary people who I am incredibly grateful to. Special thank you to Jason Caldwell, Nora Fares, John, and Chasten.

To Paul M, Kevin Matheny, centralsquareguy, KW, AG, PM, N, ED, KJ, MidNyt, RP, Caleb Waters, and all my incredible supporters on Patreon and in my Cheryl's Terrors group - thank you. Your enthusiasm, support, and belief in me means more than I can ever say.

I am lucky enough to be surrounded by friends and family who have read, supported, and encouraged my writing. To all of you, thank you, and I stand by what I said: you're the one who has to look me in the eye if you read something you didn't want to think about me writing! But also, thank you for not making it weird. I am so grateful for the special people in my life.

And finally, to the man I love more every single day: I love you. You're my everything. Thank you for standing with me, encouraging me to follow my dreams, and being my happily ever after.

About The Author

Cheryl Terra writes romantic and adult fiction with drama, sass, and a whole lot of... spice. Emotional and humorous, her books focus on contemporary relationships, inclusive characters, and happily ever afters. Living with her husband in northern Alberta, Canada, Cheryl relies on the heat between her quirky and memorable characters to help keep the gas bill down in the winter.

When she's not writing, Cheryl can be found listening to the same song(s) on repeat for hours at a time, spoiling her pets, keeping way too many house plants alive, and knitting or crocheting.

For more information and to get free books, visit Cheryl's website at **cherylterra.com**

Also By Cheryl Terra

Find all of Cheryl's books by visiting **cherylterra.com/stories**
Each series is listed in chronological order

Standalone Stories

One Little Question
When It Rains
Another Last Call
Selfish Love
What Happens In Vegas
Sore Loser
The Happiest I've Ever Been

The Unicorn Confessions

The Unicorn Confessions
Unicorn For Sale
Death of a Unicorn

The Love Across Canada Universe

Theo + Aspen:
Get Over It
More Than Words

Sean + Rick:
The Devil Made Me

Noah + Lacey:
Runaway
Waking Up
Finding Home
Of Daffodils

Collaborations with Jason Caldwell

Unseen Love
No Strings Attached
As You Wish

Get Free Books

If you want to be the first to know about new books, upcoming projects, and exclusive freebies, visit **cherylterra.com/freebies** to sign up for Cheryl's mailing list.